Embracing Family

Embracing Family

Nobuo Kojima

Translation by Yukiko Tanaka

Dalkey Archive Press
Normal · London

Originally published in Japanese as *Hoyo Kazoku* by Kodansha, 1965
Copyright © 1965 by Nobuo Kojima
Translation © 2005 by Yukiko Tanaka

First edition, 2005

Library of Congress Cataloging-in-Publication Data available.
ISBN: 1-56478-405-3

This book has been selected by the Japanese Literature Publishing Project (JLPP),
which is run by the Japanese Literature Publishing and Promotion Center (J-Lit Center)
on behalf of the Agency for Cultural Affairs of Japan.

Partially funded by a grant from the Illinois Arts Council, a state agency.

Dalkey Archive Press is a nonprofit organization located at Milner Library
(Illinois State University) and distributed in the UK by
Turnaround Publisher Services Ltd. (London).

www.dalkeyarchive.com

Printed on permanent/durable acid-free paper and bound in Canada.

Embracing Family

Prologue

Ever since Michiyo had become their maid, the Miwa household looked worse than ever. Shunsuke, the man of the house, was not pleased. The living room was a mess from the night before, and Michiyo, instead of straightening it up, was having tea in the kitchen with his wife, Tokiko, talking and laughing. Ordinarily Tokiko was fussy about having a clean, orderly house, but lately she seemed to have stopped supervising the maid altogether. This can't go on, Shunsuke said to himself. Perturbed, he walked into the kitchen, but when he spoke, the sound of his voice was gentle and he didn't even bring up the matter.

"Tokiko, that trip I told you about—you're coming with me, aren't you?"

Tokiko didn't answer. Instead, she turned to Michiyo and said, "My husband wants me to go away on a trip with him. Isn't that precious? But why would I want to go with him? It won't be any fun!" She made no attempt to disguise her hostility.

"Madam, you should go," Michiyo said. "Taking a trip together when you're no longer young can be wonderful. Think of me, a poor widow . . ."

Hearing the middle-aged woman's unctuous tone confirmed Shunsuke's sense of his house being unclean.

"It's only two nights," Shunsuke found himself pleading. "We'll be alone after I'm done with my lecture."

"I don't want to," Tokiko replied, then turned to Michiyo again. "You see, when my husband went to America, he didn't ask me to accompany him, even though I was invited too."

"If I were you, I'd go without making a fuss," Michiyo said, pretending not to have heard Tokiko's complaint.

Tokiko's laughter was shrill. "I have a better idea. Let's buy a car and we'll all go on a trip," she said.

"That sounds fun," Shunsuke said quickly, trying not to show his embarrassment. "But I'm afraid that with George, Michiyo, and the children, there won't be any space for you," Tokiko said. "You'll have to stay home."

"Oh," Shunsuke said. "Well, anyway, isn't it about time for George to get up?"

"You needn't worry about him. *I* asked Michiyo to bring him to stay with the children."

"That may be, but I'm the head of this household. I'm supposed to be responsible for what's going on here," Shunsuke said.

"Oh, I don't know about that. In America, it's the wife who takes responsibility. Aren't I right, Michiyo?"

"Yes, you are. And if the wife does a good job, her husband rewards her."

Tokiko ignored this.

A young American soldier, twenty-three years old and not much taller than Shunsuke, walked into the kitchen. Although it was a chilly morning, he wore only an undershirt on top. His light brown hair was in a GI cut, making his small head look even smaller; his thick muscled arms were covered with downy hair. He had green eyes, which would narrow when he was about to say something he thought was amusing. He was entirely unimpressive.

"This young man was so excited about coming here for Christmas, he got confused about which was his day off and he ended up

AWOL," said Michiyo in Japanese.

"I guess he likes it here."

"Of course he does. To be welcomed by a respectable Japanese family is quite an honor. Even though he's cheap, he didn't come without a gift."

"He isn't cheap," said Tokiko.

A large woman two years older than her husband, Tokiko was wearing a pink sweater; this was the first time Shunsuke had seen her in it.

"George, dear, why don't you show us how you do the Charleston," Michiyo said. Michiyo had met George through Henry, an American serviceman who was George's guardian; Henry lived with Michiyo's younger sister, who was his mistress.

"No, not now," George said. "I want to eat something."

"You can eat later. Come on, dance the Charleston for us."

George started dancing on the wooden kitchen floor.

Watching George go through his steps made Shunsuke think of the first time Tokiko danced the Charleston for him—on the tatami floor of his apartment shortly after they had met. Now this kid was in their life. They'd invited Henry and Michiyo's sister over to dinner one night; George came instead. That was over a month ago. How long was this going to go on?

"He's good," Tokiko said as George wound down. "Let's have breakfast. I'll make scrambled eggs the way he showed us the other day."

Shunsuke translated this into English for George.

George's eyes followed Tokiko as she moved about in the kitchen, and Shunsuke joined him watching her, trying to suppress his uneasiness.

George asked Shunsuke if he knew anything about Walt Whitman. He'd studied him at high school, he said, and proceeded to recite a poem in broken Japanese, gesturing with his hands:

I, you, become friends;
I was looking for you. Together we talk, eat, and sleep.

"That's from 'To a Stranger.'"

"Right," answered George. Shunsuke recited the poem in English for Tokiko, but she neither looked up nor acknowledged him.

"Madam," said Michiyo, "you should let George teach you how to dance."

"Yes, someday."

After that, Michiyo asked George to sing "Night in China."

"He's tone-deaf, but he's got the lyrics right," Tokiko remarked.

Shunsuke sang along, getting a bit carried away.

"Stop being silly," Tokiko snapped at him. "Instead of wasting time with us, you should get back to your work. You may think you're young, but you're forty-five years old."

Shunsuke got up and left. When he got to the next room, he called Tokiko.

"Yes, what is it?" she said as she went to him reluctantly.

"Well, I guess you don't want to go on the trip. But we can't buy a car for a while. I'm sorry, since you finally got your driver's license."

"You called me here to tell me that?"

Shunsuke, suddenly needing to be alone, decided to return to the translation of a play he was working on. He had to pass through his wife's room to get to his study. He was angry at himself for having sung the old song so loudly and eagerly.

After an hour, he decided to go out. As he dressed, he noticed that a button was still missing from his overcoat, the thread hanging. Several days ago he had asked Tokiko to take care of it; this time he called out to Michiyo, telling her to sew on a button.

"We couldn't find the right button. Wasn't that the reason, Madam? I'll take care of it when I can," she called back to him.

༄

Shunsuke went alone on his business trip where he spoke on the American way of life to an audience made up mostly of housewives. He was a recognized authority on this subject, having spent a year at an American university where he lectured on Japanese literature.

〰

Several weeks passed. Shunsuke came home late one evening to the sound of laughter. He heard his son Ryoichi saying, "He's back!" When Shunsuke opened the glass door to the living room, he found the group sitting in front of the television: Tokiko; Noriko, his daughter, who was a junior high school student; and George and Ryoichi, who were drinking beer. Shunsuke said hello and was about to join them when he noticed the odd face George was making. It made everyone laugh.

"No, no! It should be like this," Tokiko piped up, making a similar odd face.

Were they imitating him, making fun of him?

"Look at him! Wasn't I right?" Tokiko said, pointing at her husband.

Shunsuke felt he had to say something. "Oh, I see. It's my expression," he said, consciously changing his frown to a smile. Their imitations of him may or may not have been good, but he noted how, if his wife made fun of him like this, she had lost all restraint.

He sat for a while, watching as George proceeded to imitate a monkey, then a bleating goat. He also laughed. But he felt a chill going through his body. He could still hear everyone laughing at him as he came into the house; the sound of it reverberated in his head like a gong.

〰

Shunsuke was eating his breakfast in the kitchen as Tokiko and Michiyo discussed plans to visit Henry in the Army Hospital.

"Henry's sending a car for us, Madam," said Michiyo.

Shunsuke glanced at his calendar. "I'm free that day," he said. "I can go too. You know, I heard Henry was in the same Army unit as John Wayne. I wonder if that's true."

"George is a bit afraid of going to see that Henry by himself," said Michiyo. "Henry helped him out when he was AWOL, so he feels sheepish and obliged."

Tokiko turned to Shunsuke. "I want you to go shopping with me," she said. "I want to buy something to take with us."

"I'd be happy to," Shunsuke said. In truth he had no desire to visit Henry, but not being asked along had hurt his pride. When Tokiko asked him to help her with the shopping, he was relieved.

～

On the morning of their scheduled visit to Henry, Tokiko went to the florist. When she returned, she told Shunsuke how a young man had seemed to fancy her. "It was odd. He was wearing a red sweater; he could have been a university student. How could someone his age be interested in an older woman like me?"

When Shunsuke smiled without saying anything, she continued, "When I was getting on the bus, I noticed other people looking at me too. I guess a well-dressed woman my age attracts attention."

Shunsuke slipped on his overcoat and, getting the vase they had purchased for Henry, waited in the living room for Tokiko. Freshly powdered, she came in with Michiyo. "Oh, are you coming with us?" Tokiko asked, barely looking at him.

"Yes, I am," he replied, trying to sound casual.

～

On the way to the hospital, Tokiko spoke only to George, commenting on the passing landscape. She acted as if she was in some kind of competition and gave Shunsuke no chance to speak.

While they waited at the reception desk, Shunsuke tried to help Tokiko remove her coat. She pushed his hand away.

"But this is a Western custom," said Shunsuke.

"It looks silly!"

When an American officer glanced their way, Shunsuke grew quiet.

⌒

In Henry's room, Tokiko arranged the flowers in the vase they'd brought. Shunsuke noticed that she seemed to be gazing at George's chest; George was standing a bit on the side with an indifferent expression on his face.

"He's wearing a handsome tie, don't you think?" Shunsuke whispered.

"Tie?" Tokiko said, blushing a little. "I don't think it's anything special."

"I think it's nice. I like it," Shunsuke insisted. Then it occurred to him that Tokiko might have given George the tie. Tokiko bought all of his clothes too; realizing this made him feel a little lost.

Tokiko wanted to go to the ladies' room. Shunsuke said he had seen it at the end of the corridor, near the entrance, and he began to lead her to it. The corridor was long. At first he walked about one meter in front of her, but when he turned around, she was lagging three meters behind, walking slowly, looking out the windows, as if to say that the man in front of her was not her husband.

When Shunsuke arrived at the entrance, he only saw the men's room. He rushed to the information desk for directions only to learn that the ladies' room was next to the men's room after all. By then Tokiko was near him, having no doubt seen him hurry over to the information desk. Before he could say anything, she angrily slapped him on the hand and walked into the ladies' room; this interchange caused the American at the information desk to stare at them.

Shunsuke waited there for Tokiko, and when she emerged, he started back down the long corridor, again several meters ahead of her.

⌒

Late at night, a few days after their visit to Henry, the telephone in Shunsuke's room rang. It was George. Tokiko burst in and snatched the receiver out of Shunsuke's hand. "That call is for Ryoichi. Ask the caller to wait," she said, giving Shunsuke a sharp look. "Ryoichi, Ryoichi!" she screamed through the open door.

"It doesn't matter if I answer, does it?"

"You needn't trouble yourself."

Shocked at the tone of her voice, Shunsuke said nothing. Tokiko hung up the phone when Ryoichi picked up. It didn't seem to be an important call. Why was she so upset, especially when he was about to go away again?

One

*P*rofessor Miwa Shunsuke had just returned from a two-week lecture tour. Michiyo and Tokiko were in the kitchen, Michiyo going on about how Shunsuke had completed his translation and so must be bringing home a lot of money.

Shunsuke was relaxing in the living room, where Tokiko's dresser was kept. She was preparing to go out, so she walked in, paying Shunsuke no attention, and started to change her clothes.

"I wonder whether this one looks better," she said vacantly.

"Hmm . . . I think so," he said.

She smoothed her slip over her thighs and, twisting her hips, pulled up the tight brown skirt.

"Yes, this does look better," she said softly to her reflection in the mirror.

Shunsuke went into the backyard to practice his golf swing, using a ball attached to the club with a string.

Michiyo observed him as she pushed a mop lazily around the floor. "It might seem like a good idea, Madam, but I've heard that hitting a ball on a string develops bad habits," Michiyo said. Tokiko didn't respond. Having finished changing, she now seemed to be debating whether to go out after all.

When Shunsuke came back indoors, Michiyo asked him about his practice.

"If you can hit a ball attached to string, you'll be able to hit any ball," Shunsuke replied, keeping his eyes on Tokiko as he spoke.

Tokiko went out to visit a friend, and Shunsuke began to unpack. Michiyo approached him, saying there was something he should know, although she wasn't sure if she should tell him. He stared at her, wondering how she wanted him to respond.

"I know, I know, I know!" he shouted a moment later. Since he already knew, she might as well go ahead and tell him, he told her.

"Your wife and George . . ." Michiyo started. Shunsuke listened for a while, dazed. She didn't need to say any more. Call Tokiko and tell her to come home right away . . . No, he would call himself. He picked up the phone and dialed the number.

"Hello?" Tokiko's voice was cheerful and calm when she came to the phone. This is the tone of voice she uses in front of other people, Shunsuke thought.

⁓

As Tokiko, her head slightly bowed, approached the front door, Shunsuke went up to her and said, "Get inside! Hurry up!"

Once in the house, he followed her into the living room and pushed her onto the couch. "What did you do?!" he demanded.

"What are you talking about?" Tokiko said, trying to sit up.

What should I say, Shunsuke wondered; there was no instruction book for what to do on an occasion like this. "I know all about you two . . ." he started, "how you wouldn't let him go for three hours . . . Is that true?"

Half-lying on the couch, Tokiko looked up at him. He grabbed her hair and pulled her toward him. Then he let her fall back, and he slapped her in the face, hard, twice, three times.

"Who told you?" Tokiko said, pressing her hands to her face.

"Michiyo."

"Michiyo?"

"Yes, Michiyo. I've never liked her from the beginning anyway."

"How did she . . . ?"

"George told her."

"George?"

"He told her he was afraid what you might do next," Shunsuke yelled.

"I was going to tell you," Tokiko said softly, as if talking to herself.

Shunsuke made a hollow laugh. "What are you going to do now? Leave?" he asked.

"This is my house. I worked hard to get it built."

"It's not yours anymore."

"Please don't shout. You shouldn't shout at a time like this."

Shunsuke left Tokiko on the couch and went to the back of the house.

"Mr. Miwa," Michiyo said, coming up to him, "why did you tell her? I only told you because I thought you'd keep it to yourself. Since you give lectures on marriage and couples and relationships, I thought you would be more understanding. Madam, too, thought you'd understand. That's why—"

"That's why she did what she did. Is that what you're saying?" Shunsuke was breathing hard. "Get out of here! Pack up and leave this house!"

"I beg your pardon?" Michiyo's words were polite as always, but she glared at him, her face flushed with anger.

"I bet you were in on this too. You two talked about it all day over tea." He knew he shouldn't have said this, but he had said it anyway.

"I quit."

"Quit if you like, but remember, I fired you. You're leaving because I told you to get out. It's got nothing to do with my wife. From now on, I give the orders around here." Shunsuke spoke loudly so that Tokiko would hear. He also hoped Michiyo would be somehow appeased.

"I don't take orders from anyone," said Michiyo, looking straight at Shunsuke. Curling her lips, she jerked her shoulders back and laughed.

"When you see Henry, I want you to ask him how he could send someone like that into our house," Shunsuke said to her. He didn't really think Henry had sent him.

Shunsuke walked back into the living room. Tokiko was still sitting there, absentmindedly, with a hand on her cheek.

"You've planned this the last three months," Shunsuke said to her. "That's why you let him into our house. I always thought you believed in honesty." He felt a rush of sentimentality.

"It wasn't planned."

"Michiyo said it was."

"What a fool you are," Tokiko sighed. "You're hopeless."

"Michiyo said she suspected it for some time, but she thought I already knew it."

"She couldn't have."

"You haven't said anything. You wanted it to continue, didn't you? How could you ask me which skirt to wear?"

"If you say such things, and Michiyo hears them, you're proving what she said is true."

"What do you mean?"

"Don't you see? If both you and Michiyo say the same thing, that means I really did plan it. And that makes you a fool. After all, the thing that pushes a wife into something like this is her husband's inability to satisfy her. We must look pathetic."

"So that's it . . ." Shunsuke mumbled.

"You just lost face, and you don't even know it. I was going to tell you about George at the right time. But it's your fault this happened, and if I stay with you, other things may happen too." Tokiko was quiet for a bit, deep in thought, then said, "It's too late now. Michiyo will make fun of us, I'm sure."

Tokiko then went to the foyer, put her shoes on, and left the house. Shunsuke hurried to catch up with her, walking alongside her for a while. Then he took her arm and led her back to the house.

⁓

At dinner that evening, Ryoichi asked where George was.

"He treated me badly, so I've decided not to let him come here anymore," Tokiko answered.

"Really? What did he do?"

"He said bad things about me, things that weren't true. I don't want a person like that in our home."

"When was that? Was it after he went to the movie with you?"

"You don't have to know the details."

"He stayed here night before last, and you went to the movie with him yesterday, so it must have been after that," Ryoichi persisted. "I was nice to him. I let him sleep in my bed . . ."

"This is why I don't like Americans," Noriko remarked.

"That's enough," Shunsuke said, sounding as casual as he could manage.

⁓

Shunsuke started experiencing physical pain after he learned about Tokiko and George. It was as if someone had kicked him in the groin. The pain was concentrated in his lower abdomen and even caused his heart to ache. He felt this pain whenever Tokiko approached him outside the house, whenever she said, "this is my house," whenever she said, "I'm not your possession." It hurts, it hurts so bad, he said to himself.

As he sat anxious and still in his room, he could hear Tokiko spreading out her bedding, then turning the pages of a magazine.

"Oh, it hurts," Shunsuke said loudly.

Tokiko said nothing.

"It really hurts," he said again, opening the door to her room.

She looked at him from head to toe, not saying a word.

"It's killing me, the pain here."

"Don't be ridiculous," Tokiko said, almost whispering.

"Here! It hurts."

"Turn around. I'm going to undress."

"Go ahead, do it in front of me."

"No."

"All right, but be quick," said Shunsuke. When Tokiko got into her bed, Shunsuke turned around. She was looking up at him.

"Michiyo told me that on that day you were drinking with George and Ryoichi, and that after a while, you said it was time to go to bed. You told Ryoichi to sleep in my room, and you went to Ryoichi's room, where George was. And you turned the light off. I heard a lot more in detail," Shunsuke went on, giving Tokiko no chance to interrupt.

"Don't talk so loud. The children will hear," Tokiko said in low voice. "I know you're going to keep bringing this up, but don't shout."

"If you're so concerned about the children, why did you use Ryoichi's bed?" Shunsuke said sadly. When she made no response, he said, "What are you thinking now, Tokiko?"

"I don't understand why he lied," she muttered, her face half buried in the quilt.

"Who?"

"George, of course."

Shunsuke was silent for a while, then spoke quietly. "Tokiko, you really are important to me. You are my wife and the mother of my children."

"If I'm so important, why did you hit me!" Tokiko shouted.

"Not so loud." It was Shunsuke's turn to tell her to keep her voice down. His breathing was labored. He went on, "You say it doesn't make sense, but it does. The first time we slept together, remember, it was you who turned the light off. You did the same thing without realizing."

"I just don't understand why he lied."

Shunsuke got the feeling that Tokiko was not just playing innocent.

"You told him not to tell anyone?"

"Yes, that's what I don't understand. I wonder if he really did tell Michiyo," Tokiko said, preoccupied.

"I'm in pain, and you're acting like *you* need help," Shunsuke said suddenly, holding his lower abdomen.

"I won't say any more if you don't want me to."

"Tell me everything, Tokiko." Shunsuke got into his wife's bed, and when she tried to pull away, he grabbed her shoulder. She struggled, but he was firm. "Now, tell me," he demanded.

"I will, I will . . . Just don't grab me like that. Hold me the way you used to."

"The way I used to?" He did as Tokiko asked. "Now, tell me."

"Hold me tight. It's easier to talk when you hold me like that," said Tokiko, the tone of her voice quite different, as if she was intoxicated. She began to tell him everything. They fell into a litany, where whatever Tokiko said Shunsuke repeated back to her:

"You said, 'Let's go to bed,' meaning it was time to go to sleep, and you think he misunderstood . . . When you were brushing your teeth and he came up behind you, you told him to wait, which he might have taken to mean wait in the bedroom . . . After you got into bed, you heard a loud noise from his room, and when you went to see what was the matter, he pulled you into his bed, and it was he, not you, who turned the light off . . . You couldn't fight him off because if you raised your voice, it would wake the children . . . You didn't keep him for three hours; he wouldn't let you go . . . Is that what you're saying? But according to Michiyo, you surprised him the next morning by returning to his room and kissing him."

"That's nonsense. You've been taken in by that woman," said Tokiko. "I went back to make sure I hadn't left anything behind. You can believe that, can't you?" she whispered.

"Then he's a bastard and a liar," Shunsuke said angrily, although he still harbored doubts about her story.

"I wonder if he's a coward, and he told those lies because he was scared," said Tokiko, who then added, sighing, "but he was good at making it impossible to get away."

This made Shunsuke want to laugh, but at the same time it was like the sting of a whip.

"How did he do it?" Shunsuke asked after a few moments.

Tokiko started to explain, hesitated, then stopped. "We've had enough, haven't we? So don't make me to say any more. It really is better with you—with a Japanese, you know," she said.

Shunsuke touched her body.

"He did all kinds of things . . . I want you to do the same . . ."

When it was over, unsuccessfully as he had feared, Tokiko uttered a faint cry. Peeling his body off hers, Shunsuke got up, ran into his room, and collapsed on his bed. He heard Tokiko yawn.

↲

Shunsuke lay wide-awake, listening to the sound of Tokiko's breathing as she slept. A couple of hours later, still unable to sleep, he moaned loudly, hoping Tokiko would hear.

"What should we do?" she said after a few moments.

"It's because of you that I can't do it," he said.

"It's not my fault."

"Yes, it is. Do you remember," said Shunsuke, going into Tokiko's room and sitting on her bed, "the time when we went to the seaside resort? I came back early because I had some work to do, and you stayed on with the children. You had a good time with those college students; one of them came to visit you afterward, and you went with him to a coffee shop. You told me you were going to introduce him to a girl, but I knew you had written him a letter; you'd hidden it behind the bookcase. You went with him because, secretly, you were looking for something. The first time we had this problem was right after that."

It had been their first vacation since the children were born. Tokiko complained that the kitchen where they were staying wasn't clean and the that bathroom smelled, but on the beach she eased up, walking slowly, seeming to forget about her husband. One day, when she and Shunsuke were in the ocean together, Tokiko began to swim toward a large black rock two hundred meters away. Shunsuke didn't want to swim so far, so he called out to her to turn back, but Tokiko ignored him and kept on going.

When Shunsuke got back to shore, their daughter Noriko was playing alone. Ryoichi was nowhere to be seen; alarmed, Shunsuke began to search the beach for him. Then, suddenly, the boy stood up in the shallow water. Relieved, Shunsuke looked out toward Tokiko and saw her climbing onto the rock. He did not take his eyes from her the whole time she sat on it. After Tokiko swam back, she told Noriko and Ryoichi how far she'd gone, but she said nothing to Shunsuke.

Before they went back to the city, Tokiko wanted to go for another long swim, and Shunsuke offered to join her. Tokiko responded with a look of displeasure; she seemed to want to be left alone—at the seaside at least. But why did she have to glare at me like that? Shunsuke asked himself. He had never interfered with her life; he had always deferred to her wishes even when he disagreed.

It must have been then that Tokiko swam to the rock with the college student.

Tokiko looked at her husband, bewildered and uncertain of his intentions in unearthing the ancient incident.

At the end of that summer, Shunsuke recalled, Tokiko suddenly wanted to have a new house built. He wondered if the two events were connected: if the beach incident was related to the fact that Tokiko, after making Shunsuke find a way to finance it, had managed to have the house completed within six months. Had she been trying to reach out for the happiness of a stable home, or had she simply wanted to show how capable she was?

"You've always been like this, I see it now. You've doubted me all along. That's why things like this happen. You're right, I've been dissatisfied," she said, then yelled out: "Yes, dissatisfied!"

"I've done the same things George did to you with another woman. And I was able to please her."

"When was that?" Tokiko raised herself up.

"Right before I went abroad. She was married."

"Well then, you're paying for that now. Tell me what you did with her. I want to know."

"I didn't fall in love with her. When I was in bed with her, I was actually thinking about you," Shunsuke said, picturing George's young, virile body.

"You must have gone to a hotel. That's what I should have done. Who would want to do it in their own house? You accused me of using Ryoichi's bed. Well, I didn't want to. If we had gone somewhere else, I might have enjoyed it."

"Women are different from men."

"How? The worst thing was you didn't have any feeling for the woman," Tokiko said, turning to face him. "Try and do to me what you did to her. Go ahead! You can't, can you? You're being punished. It's a punishment," Tokiko laughed.

Shunsuke moved away from her. "Then what Michiyo said is true," he said. "You planned to keep on sleeping with him. You must like the kind of man who brags about it afterwards."

"I don't dislike him, although he's a coward. If he was a decent man, and if I was younger, I would have left this house and gone with him," Tokiko said, deliberately pausing, as if examining her thoughts. "Even to America. Or wherever."

"I see," said Shunsuke, getting up and leaving.

⌒

Shunsuke waited for the morning to come like a sick person waits for morning.

When it got light, he went outdoors. Why am I looking at the garden when I have no interest in it? he asked himself. Why am I looking at the garden when I feel totally lost, as if help might be out here? He looked at the azalea, he looked at the trees—the cedar, the crape myrtle, the plum, the horse chestnut, the persimmon. Tokiki had said, "I'm not your possession," but Shunsuke found he had little passion for the things he possessed.

The crape myrtle had red blooms, and the water lilies in the large ceramic pot were about to open. Three sparrows, no, four, were picking away at the ground. Two dogs were loitering on the other side of the hedge; one was theirs. The houses nearby seemed to blend together, one indistinguishable from the next.

When flowers pollinate, is there a sense of joy, like the feeling a man and a woman have when they embrace? There must be, Shunsuke thought, feeling jealous. Even a stone, or clay, might experience fulfillment and purpose. If that was the case, how much better they were than him and Tokiko, who had just turned her body away from him in bed.

There was water in another ceramic pot in the garden. Why do I care that there is water in it? he asked himself. Water was such a trivial thing.

⌒

Shunsuke found himself standing beside Tokiko. She looked faded. With Michiyo gone, she had prepared breakfast herself, and now she too stared out at the garden. It's awkward to be alone with her like this, he thought. What was she thinking?

"Can a man do it with a woman even if he doesn't love her?" she asked softly without turning to face him.

"You think he did it because he was in love with you? I don't know. I don't know what you two talked about. I don't know anything about you and him." As soon as he said this, Shunsuke realized that Tokiko was thinking about something entirely different; he felt the pain in his groin. "Perhaps he found you attractive," he said; he was surprised at his words.

"You're the only one who thinks so," said Tokiko. When she turned around to face him, he saw her cheeks wet with tears.

"That's not true. Just the other day you told me the young man at the florist was interested in you. You're attractive, really," he said, wondering why they continued to carry on this kind of conversation.

"I need to talk to someone about this. Where should I go? Do you know?"

"Well," Shunsuke mumbled, not knowing how to respond. "If you did say anything to anyone, you might regret it later. So, even if you want to, you'd better not."

Tokiko nodded, sitting down.

Shunsuke became aware at that moment that changes were occurring inside him.

He was gazing at Tokiko's neckline, at her crossed legs, and even though he had spoken quietly, he did not feel calm. This neck and these legs had been caressed by a young man, he thought; it was possible that she had planned it. Instead of anger, however, he felt overwhelmed by the blinding realization that before him was a woman.

Had she only wanted all along to acknowledge a light she felt glimmering inside herself, and to have others acknowledge it too? And had he been refusing to do so? Did he think it was absurd, and so looked away? Why? Or perhaps it was that very light that drew him towards her.

Shunsuke gazed at Tokiko—the veins in her arms, the glow of her skin, her eyelashes as her eyes opened and closed, the structure of her bones, her neck and shoulder lines, her stomach, her breasts, one slightly larger than the other, her rather long, sturdy, well-shaped legs. He observed all this anew, as if with the eyes of a creator, and he was amazed at the wholeness of this person who no longer clung to him, who was now independent of him. Shunsuke wanted to escape from this state of mind.

I must rebuild my home, he thought.

Shunsuke was tormented, thinking of Tokiko's body lying in bed with George, of the noises they made.

"Did you let him in our house because I didn't take you abroad with me?" he whispered.

"What . . . ? Because you didn't take me . . . ? Oh, that. Perhaps . . . You may be right. But I feel suffocated. You suffocate me with the way you think. Whenever you say something to me, I end up feeling you're right. Thoughts that I've never had become convincing. And that's your fault. I feel like you're always telling me what to do. It was you who told me to let him into our house . . . Yes, that's it."

"I didn't know what was going on, and besides, even if I did, I couldn't have prevented it."

"But you see, don't you? Something about you made me think you were telling me to do it. It's the same whether you actually said it or not."

"I want to get one thing straight, Tokiko. Did you do it because I didn't take you to America with me? Did you drag that man into this house to bring America to you?"

"Yes. I did. You're right. Since you think so, it must be true. Didn't you think it was going to happen the first time we met him? So I went ahead and did it."

"So that's the reason you made him your pet."

"Oh, God! Now I don't feel like going to my dancing lessons anymore."

Dancing lessons at your age, Shunsuke thought, but he kept it to himself.

～

From where he stood on deck of the ship, Shunsuke could see his wife and children amid the crowd at the pier. He flung streamers to them, as did the other passengers, most of whom were not Japanese; the children, stretching out their arms to him, seemed to be screaming, "Throw one to Mom!" Between where he stood on the ship and his family at the pier, the distance was great.

That was the second time Shunsuke had viewed Tokiko from a distance. The first time had been when, returning from the war, he was approaching the village his family had been evacuated to. Walking on the open road alongside the stream that led into the village, he saw Tokiko in *monpe* pantaloons coming out of the temple. She was a hundred meters away and just stood there, waiting for him to come closer. He couldn't run to her because of the heavy backpack he was wearing, so he continued to walk slowly toward her. Why didn't she come running to him?

Standing on the deck of the ship, Shunsuke wondered why Tokiko didn't ask to be taken along. Although he was relieved not to have been asked, he would have let her come if she had. The ship headed slowly out to sea, and in a half hour, from Shunsuke's vantage point, the crowd standing on the pier had shrunk to a miniscule cluster.

A few days later, photographs were displayed on board, selling for two dollars each. Among them Shunsuke found an enlarged snapshot of his family. Tokiko was standing with a child on either side of her; there were tears in her eyes. Usually Shunsuke laughed when he saw his wife in tears, but not this time.

Two days before his departure, Tokiko had come to his room and sat down next to him. "What are we going to do about the children?" she said. "We haven't talked about them at all."

"You can write and ask me. But you should've told me not to leave instead of complaining now," he said.

"You don't understand," Tokiko said, starting to weep. Shunsuke realized that she might be right. Tokiko, who usually showed her affection by talking high-handedly, was now wiping away her tears with the sleeve of her blouse. This is not what I wanted, he thought; what he wanted was for her to express herself gently and to have the attitude of a compliant wife willing to go along with her husband's decisions.

"You don't understand how a woman feels at all," she said again, sobbing as she pounded her knees with her fist.

"I don't have time to talk now. Besides, I'm not going because I want to," Shunsuke replied sulkily.

"That's not what I'm talking about. You ruin every chance a woman has to feel happy. That's what I mean."

Shunsuke grimaced because he couldn't think of anything to say.

He had been seeing the other woman until the week before. He had kept seeing her with the slight hope that there might be something in it for him, but their assignations always ended in disappointment, making him feel he had wasted his time. Once, when the woman asked why he was always so sullen, he answered that he was too busy to be otherwise. "In that case, why do you go on seeing me?" she asked.

Tokiko's claim that he didn't understand a woman's feelings struck Shunsuke like a thunderbolt. In effect she was saying the same thing the other woman had. He hadn't been paying much attention to either of them. What shocked him, however, weren't Tokiko's words but the fact she had dared to speak them. That she had to refer to herself as being a woman was also surprising.

Tokiko's face in the snapshot brought her words back to Shunsuke, and he could not easily forget either her face or her words.

Her weekly letters to him said nothing more about it. Instead, they were filled with her concerns about the children. When he read her letters, he often felt dejected, not finding any tenderness in them. And when he returned home, the first thing he noticed was the irritation written on her face.

"I can't sleep unless all the shutters are closed, and even then sometimes I stay awake till morning," she said. The night of his return she slept soundly.

"It's such a difference, your being home. That means you're important to me after all. I'll have to be nice to you from now on," she said in the morning.

He slept in her room and made love to her after some relaxed conversation. Prior to his trip abroad, they only had sex when Tokiko came to him. Sometimes he waited for her in his room, but she didn't come; at other times she came after his desire had left him, and sometimes even when he did feel like it, his body wouldn't function, as if it belonged to someone else. When he'd had something to drink and slipped into Tokiko's bed just to satisfy himself, as if she were a prostitute, he seemed more capable of the physical act.

Ironically, Shunsuke had not felt uneasy about sex with Tokiko when he was seeing the other woman. He had felt guilty but also more affectionate toward her. He wouldn't really pursue her, but he felt relaxed; whatever Tokiko said did not disturb him. Their relationship had been like a quiet stream, and when she came to his room, he had been able to satisfy her.

When Tokiko was planning their new house, Shunsuke had assumed, without thinking, that they would share a bedroom. When work on the house was completed, he found that they were still separate, side-by-side. Tokiko refused to give up her bedroom to make it theirs.

"That's what you say, but it won't work," she had said then. "As soon as you've satisfied yourself, you'll want to go to your own room; you wouldn't be able to sleep in the same room with me. Besides, if I wanted to talk to you about something, you'd just shut me up. You're never interested in what I have to say."

"Is that really true?" Shunsuke had said, but secretly he thought she might be right. Although he wasn't the type who closed his ears to the opinions of others, he knew he often tuned her out. By then, Tokiko had stopped gossiping about the other housewives and talked instead about the children's education and how to cultivate a more sophisticated life. Still competitive, she made endless plans, and when they didn't materialize, she complained. Shunsuke tuned her out because she wouldn't listen to what he said anyway. Watching Tokiko made him feel uneasy, and only when they made love did he feel that they had made contact with each other. He had been afraid that she'd sense this, that he couldn't insist they share a bedroom.

"You became disappointed in me after I returned from abroad, but you didn't want to say so. Instead you decided to ignore me, is that it?"

"I guess so. Whatever you say, you are always right."

"Please don't twist my words, Tokiko. This is important."

"It isn't important," Tokiko said, shaking her head. "I don't care about the reason."

"You said you didn't want to see me disillusioned with myself."

"Why do you want to know the reason? If I tell you, you'd be more upset," she snapped. "But I do want to say something to Michiyo. And I want to see George, too . . . There's something I need to find out," she added, sighing.

⌐

That evening, Shunsuke was scheduled to give a public lecture on "Family Life in Western Countries." As he was leaving the auditorium after the event, he felt the same sharp pain in his groin. It was so bad he had to sit down on the curb until the pain passed. He then walked to the nearest doctor's office.

"I've had this pain; it's like my heart is being squeezed. Then the pain moves down to here," Shunsuke explained, pointing to his groin. When the doctor, a man in his late fifties, didn't say anything, Shunsuke continued, "My wife has caused me some distress, and this symptom is related to that. I feel the pain whenever I think of it."

It seemed the doctor was trying not to smile. "I'll give you some tranquilizers. I think that'll take care of it, but if you need more help, you should come back. Your type tends to have problems with the autonomic nervous system. Here, take one of these pills now and sit down for a while," the doctor said, then went into the next room.

After a while, Shunsuke stood up and called out, "I'm feeling fine now, doctor."

"I thought so. Take another pill if it happens again," the doctor said, sounding vaguely amused.

Surprised that the pain had stopped so suddenly, Shunsuke went straight home.

꒛

"Is Father back yet?" he heard Tokiko's voice as he entered the house.

"He's back, Mom. Don't worry," Ryoichi replied.

"Really? I didn't think he'd be back this early."

When Shunsuke went into the living room, Tokiko was lying on the couch, watching television with her son and daughter. She yawned, and said to Shunsuke, "Well, we have to find another maid."

꒛

Around midnight, Shunsuke jumped out of bed and changed into street clothes, but in order to get to the front door, he had to go through Tokiko's room. As usual, Tokiko's face was half covered by the quilt. A strange light flickered in her eyes.

"Where are you going?"

"I don't know. Nowhere in particular. I'm just going for a walk."

"You'd better put your walking shoes on. You have to remember you're not young anymore."

"Shoes?"

He put on his walking shoes, went down the steps outside the house and opened the gate. We've spent a lot of money on this house, with these steps and this gate, Shunsuke thought. But for what, and what are we doing?

The moment he stepped outside the gate, he realized he didn't really want to go for a walk. The house next door, with light in the windows, loomed in front of him. Which way should he turn? When he started down the slope, he felt something warm and moist fall on his forehead. It was a large raindrop: first one, then a few. In early spring this was rare.

Shunsuke was reminded of an autumn day in America when he went for a walk through the suburb he was staying in. He looked at the lawns and houses and thought of Tokiko. Whenever he felt relaxed, he wished she were with him. Then, as he continued on his way, something hard fell on his head. It was a walnut.

~

When he answered the phone the next afternoon, Shunsuke found himself completely unprepared: it was George.

"How are you, Mr. Miwa?" he asked, sounding as if nothing had happened.

"Just fine!" Shunsuke shouted. His response was ludicrous, but he couldn't come up with anything else to say.

"Who is it?" Tokiko asked, racing into the room. Shunsuke was annoyed, but he wouldn't have liked it if she hadn't come running in, either.

"What is he saying?" Tokiko moved closer. Shunsuke thought they must look like a couple excited over an invitation to a party.

"He wants to see me, and he's telling me where we should meet," he told Tokiko, intentionally not covering the mouthpiece.

"I'll come with you."

"You will?" Why would she want to do that? If she spoke English, she would insist on going by herself. She doesn't want me to meet George alone because she's afraid I might do something crazy or because she's worried I'll get into trouble. Maybe she wants to go for George's sake. Shunsuke wasn't sure which. He was perplexed that she wanted to go along. He didn't trust George, but he didn't trust Tokiko either. He wanted the two of them to confront each other, but in fact what he really wanted, cruelly, was for the three of them to meet.

"It's raining. You'll need your raincoat. I'll take an umbrella," Shunsuke said to Tokiko.

She nodded. "What should I wear?" she asked.

"How about your light green suit? And fix your hair." Shunsuke had never advised Tokiko about details like this, but now it seemed only natural.

"All right, but you'd better change your tie," Tokiko said.

"How about the navy blue one?"

"That'll be fine. Do we have enough time to make it?"

"Don't worry about him," Shunsuke snapped.

"That's not what I meant."

After he instructed the taxi driver to go to Ginza, Shunsuke couldn't stop talking: too much road construction was going on these days; this road had already been repaired once this year, three times in the past several years; Americans drive on the highway sixty miles per hour. As he rattled on, he addressed a silent question to Tokiko, who sat beside him quietly: "What are you thinking now, Tokiko?"

There had been times when Shunsuke was afraid that the husband of the woman he was involved with would come to see him. If he had, it was clear what he would've wanted; what Shunsuke knew, however, was that he would only smile at him. The husband wouldn't smile back, of course. What would Shunsuke do then? To the unsmiling eyes of the husband, he couldn't keep on smiling. Because then his smile would have a different meaning. What would he say, what would he do? He had no idea.

Now, Shunsuke understood the situation he was in but still couldn't think of anything to say or do. This meant, in short, that he couldn't find a good enough reason to condemn the other man. Supposing one could kill on an occasion like this, whom would he kill?

The taxi dropped them off at the entrance to the D Hotel, where there were a few foreigners entering and leaving. Shunsuke took Tokiko to the hotel's Wild Cat Café, where loud music was playing, and he told her to wait there. He then went to the bar in the basement where George was sitting in a far corner, staring at the entrance. He's on his guard, Shunsuke thought. He then realized that he was walking with exaggeratedly large steps, and his shoulders perked up.

"My wife is waiting at a place near here. I want to hear what you have to say before she sees you," Shunsuke said, taking off his coat. George asked him what he wanted to drink. "A beer will do," Shunsuke replied. Although he had intended to talk softly, there was an aggressive edge in the tone of his voice. The face of the man he'd thought a great deal of and tried to forget, the face of the man who'd touched Tokiko's face and body to give her pleasure, was in front of him. That the man sat there, looking as uneasy as he did, struck Shunsuke as comical.

"Where's your wife?"

"I told you she's waiting elsewhere," Shunsuke said more rudely than he'd intended. He was angry at George's using the word "wife."

"You look heartbroken, Mr. Miwa. You must not be well. I am really sorry."

"You're sorry! What an extraordinary thing to say!" Shunsuke exclaimed, enunciating his words, hoping to sound high-handed. Some foreign customers in the bar turned to look their way.

"You sound very angry, but you don't need to be. Nothing happened between your wife and me."

"Nothing happened? Are you making fun of me?" Shunsuke felt the familiar pain starting.

"There was nothing. You should believe me and stop worrying, Mr. Miwa."

"Hey, you!" Shunsuke shouted. He had heard GIs use this expression.

"Well, then, you're forcing me to tell you the truth," George said, smiling wryly. "But I warn you, it'll only make you feel worse."

"Why's that?"

"Because she was the one who forced me into it."

"She forced you? Tell me. I want to hear it all."

"It'll only make you angrier."

"All right then, come with me to where my wife's waiting, and you can tell us both." Shunsuke stood up, grabbed his raincoat and headed to the door with George following.

"What about the check?"

"You pay," Shunsuke said.

"I have to meet a friend."

"Too bad. Tell whoever it is you're suddenly busy." Shunsuke didn't lower his voice, even though he knew that they were now the focus of everyone in the bar. Shunsuke stood next to George while he made a call to his friend; he wanted to show that he wouldn't let him get away.

It was still raining outside.

"I don't have an umbrella," said the young American with a small head, looking helpless.

"A soldier doesn't need an umbrella," Shunsuke said and walked ahead without sharing his. Realizing how much his English had improved since he'd known George, he smiled to himself.

Walking to the café where Tokiko was waiting, Shunsuke looked back to make sure George was following. George kept his face turned toward the street, shaking his head from time to time as if to say that the man walking in front of him was a big nuisance. For Shunsuke, the entire situation was wretched.

Tokiko was waiting at a corner table where Shunsuke had left her. Shunsuke and George sat down across from her. First, Tokiko looked straight at George, and then she asked her husband in Japanese, "How did it go?"

Shunsuke told her what George had said.

"That's a lie," she muttered without taking her eyes off George. "Ask him why he lied to Michiyo, why he said say things that weren't true."

Shunsuke translated this for George.

"No, no. Do you believe her?"

"I don't believe either of you, but why did you spread it around?"

"I'm scared of her. She's crazy."

"Crazy? Scared? Fine," said Shunsuke reprovingly after he translated it for Tokiko. "Then I'll have Tokiko say exactly how it went with you two, to find out whether you were forced or not. If her story isn't true, you can say so."

Tokiko described the night in detail, and Shunsuke translated. While her story contradicted George's almost entirely, it was clear that Tokiko had been in bed with George for a long time, being caressed by him. Shunsuke, speaking loudly now, put his hand in George's face and shoved, almost making him fall out of his chair.

"Stop it!" Tokiko said.

Jazz was playing in the cafe, but here too everyone was looking at them.

"Ask him if he feels responsible, and tell him that I feel responsible for my part," Tokiko said; Shunsuke translated.

"Responsible? To whom?" George exclaimed. "If I ever feel responsible to anyone, it's to my parents and my country."

When he heard this, Shunsuke's anger flared again and he shoved George a second time before he translated for Tokiko.

"Tell him I despise Americans," Tokiko said.

"Why does she despise me?" George asked, shrugging.

"You have to admire his logic and the way he sticks to his story," Tokiko cried out in amazement.

Shunsuke looked at her, surprised at her remark.

"I've had enough. This is all I need to hear," she added, urging Shunsuke to end the conversation and leave.

George, who was waiting for Shunsuke to say something, stood up and followed the two toward the door. While George was using the men's room, Shunsuke paid the bill and waited for him outside.

"Go home, Yankee! Go home!" he shouted at George when he came out of the café. The words came out of his mouth involuntarily.

"I'm going home in a month," George replied and walked away.

Shunsuke opened the umbrella for Tokiko, and they walked away in the opposite direction.

"He got pale when you pinned him down, didn't he?" Tokiko said.

"Yes, he did," replied Shunsuke, trembling with excitement. The pain was coming back. He still didn't know what he should have done.

⌐

After dinner, Shunsuke and Tokiko stayed in the kitchen talking.

"Oh, no, it's eleven already," Tokiko said suddenly, looking up at the clock. "I didn't know it was this late. You shouldn't have made me talk like this." She sounded sad.

Shunsuke put his hand over her mouth. When she shook her head, he pretended he was going to choke her.

"You're crazy, you're a murderer!" she shouted. "No matter what kind of bastard he is, he's better than you. If I was younger, I would've gone with him."

It took an hour for her to calm down.

ر

When Shunsuke finished his breakfast the next morning, Tokiko was still in bed. "Are you feeling better now," she asked, looking up at him.

Tokiko did not leave her bed until evening. When she said that Michiyo was supposed to come by later that day, Shunsuke asked if she was going to straighten out the discrepancies in Michiyo's story. Yes, that was her intention, she said.

While they waited for Michiyo to show up, Shunsuke took a bath.

"Honey—" Tokiko said, opening the bathroom door and peeking in at Shunsuke washing himself.

"What is it?" he asked, turning his head and looking over his shoulder at her.

"How's the bath?"

"Fine."

"You haven't rinsed your back very well."

"Haven't I?"

"You should do it better than that."

Several years before, on one or two occasions, Tokiko had peeked into the bathroom like this, asking him if he wanted her to pour water down his back. Now, she was talking to him in a deliberately rough tone, gazing intently at his nakedness.

"Well, I'll close the door if you don't need me," she said.

Tokiko took her bath afterward. Realizing that he wanted to see her naked body just as she had wanted to see his, Shunsuke opened the bathroom door and, without saying anything, watched her bathe. He waited to see if she would say something.

"I have to wash my hair," she said.

⁓

Later that evening Michiyo arrived. Wearing a dress that Shunsuke recognized as a gift from Tokiko, the former maid walked into the living room and sat down smugly on the couch without saying a word. Here's the man who lost his composure and hit his wife just the other day and now he sits with his head held high as if he was a confident husband, she seemed to be saying to herself; he is even more despicable than his adulterous wife, but when and how did these two make up?

"I met George yesterday at his request. I took Tokiko with me," Shunsuke began.

"That's funny. George said someone called him last night and frightened him. So it wasn't Mrs. Miwa."

"You mean she's still . . ." Shunsuke said, the words slipping out. Getting back to the question at hand, Shunsuke told Michiyo that according to George, he had said nothing about Tokiko's not letting him go for hours, that Michiyo had exaggerated the story. George wanted to make that point very clear, Shunsuke said.

"But Mr. Miwa, they say a woman cannot have sex unless she is attracted to the man. You don't agree?"

"For your own sake, you'd better not say things like that."

"Well, I'd better go now. I don't see any point in continuing this conversation," Michiyo said, standing up abruptly.

"I think there's something funny going on between George and your sister," Tokiko said suddenly. When Shunsuke tried to stop her, Tokiko became agitated.

"My sister and I are not as shameless as you may think," Michiyo replied. "I know I'm not good at cleaning the house, but . . ."

"I wonder what's going on," Tokiko snickered.

"This has been a good lesson for me," Michiyo said firmly. "George wants to go ice-skating with my sister. We're trying to cheer him up because we feel sorry for him." She paused, then continued aggressively, "Mr. Miwa, I told Henry what happened, and he said that since your wife and George aren't children, you should settle it among yourselves. He was angry with George, though, and said if this had happened in the States, George couldn't complain even if he was shot. But he said he thought your wife should take responsibility for her own actions."

The last sentence shocked Shunsuke.

Michiyo left the Miwa house. Shunsuke and Tokiko watched her as she walked off, shaking her hips as in a hurry.

"Well, I guess that's it. Nothing more to say. Michiyo will tell everyone about us, you'll see. And what is she? Nothing but a housemaid."

᠎

"Say," said Tokiko, addressing her husband; she lay with a blanket over her and her legs stretched out under the *kotatsu* foot warmer. Shunsuke was lying next to her. It was a chilly evening.

"What?" said Shunsule. Tokiko's foot was on his, her toes grasping his.

"You should be able to ignore these things. You should stay calm and see the whole thing as comic. After all, you're an expert on foreign literature."

"Comic?"

"To think that it's tragic is old-fashioned. Isn't that the way you think anyway?"

Shunsuke thought this over.

"I went to see *The Grass Is Greener*," Tokiko said, changing the subject.

"With him?"

"The children went too. I didn't mean to see that particular movie, but I thought a comedy would be best. George and the children agreed."

"What was it about?"

"It's about a nouveau riche American who goes to stay at an old English manor and falls in love with the wife of the owner."

"What does the husband do?"

"The husband and the lover have a duel, and when the husband gets hurt, the wife rushes to him to take care of him."

"You can't call it a comedy if they have a duel," Shunsuke said, trying to appear calm even though he was shaken. He sensed something was going on in Tokiko.

"But the person who shot the husband was the butler, injuring him in the arm just a little bit. He had emptied both pistols beforehand."

"The American runs away then?"

"Yes."

"And the couple make up?"

"No, it doesn't end that way. They have an argument, and the wife says she's going to leave him."

"I see. And does the husband have a mistress?"

"There's a woman who's been after him, but he isn't interested in her."

"I still don't see how it's a comedy."

"You should go see it."

Shunsuke felt like laughing.

"You should be able to laugh. You rarely laugh with me, only with your male friends. You used to laugh, you used to make them laugh. You also laughed when no one else laughed."

"I can't deny that."

"I didn't like that about you, but it's good that you laughed like that. You should be able to laugh this time, too."

The title of the movie meant that the grass in someone else's yard always looks greener, that things belonging to other people always seem better than your own. So, Shunsuke thought, maybe Tokiko's going to a movie like that with George triggered their affair; the comic lightness of the movie might have had something to do with it.

"I'm disgusted with the whole thing. I don't even want to think about it. I'm an old woman, as you know."

"No, you're not," Shunsuke said emphatically and moved his foot away from hers.

"We've got to get back to a more normal life. You shouldn't be so attractive to me as you are now." Lying on the floor, she stared at him.

"Mom . . ." Noriko said, walking into the living room. When Shunsuke heard the word "Mom," he was filled with anger at Tokiko.

⌒

Shunsuke was walking with Tokiko, who was wearing a hat. They were inside a huge building in Chicago, or maybe it was New York; it may have been a train station. The interior of the building was gray and orange. When he looked out a window, he saw empty space below. Then a building began to grow in that empty space, and it seemed that he and Tokiko were supposed to spend the night in that building. On top of a hill, beyond other buildings, was a grove of pine trees. Shunsuke and Tokiko began to sway. Back in the building, they sat on a sofa, waiting; he didn't know why, but he heard a voice. He might have been expecting it, as he held Tokiko's hand.

"Mr. and Mrs. Miwa, the execution will take place in one hour," a metallic voice said from a loudspeaker.

"Who's going to be executed?" he said, standing up.

"Your children."

"Why? That's ridiculous! Did you hear that, Tokiko?"

Tokiko gazed at him. They hadn't seen their children for a long time because they had left them somewhere far away. And now, within an hour, they were going to be executed.

"We must go and request that the sentence to be reduced," Shunsuke said. He went to the front desk and asked where they should go; he was given a room number. As he climbed up the stairs, he looked back and saw that Tokiko was gone. He could not think of any reason why his children had to be executed, but it didn't occur to him to ask that the execution be halted; he only wanted the sentence reduced. Tokiko did not suggest otherwise. While he looked for the room, time passed quickly. He asked a passerby where the room was, and learned that the room he wanted was in the annex. The building he was in, then, had to be the department store where he and Tokiko were supposed to be shopping.

Shunsuke shopped alone. He wanted to buy a pair of hiking boots and sought out the section where boots were sold. He bought a pair, realizing that he had wanted to walk in a sure-footed way for some time. His wife made him feel that way. But now he couldn't find her anywhere. He looked outside, and there she was in the sky above the pine tree, writing a letter with her back to him. He tried to read what she was writing but she stood up and hid the letter. Then she disappeared among the other pine trees.

Shunsuke crossed the street and arrived at the annex. Over an hour had passed. He began to wail. He heard Tokiko's voice, but he could not move his head; it was glued to the pillow. He lay still, thinking that if he had a chance, he would run.

"What's the matter?" Tokiko said.

Shunsuke could hardly open his eyes. "I don't know," he said. "I've forgotten. Is it daytime now, or is it still night?"

"It's dawn," Tokiko replied. "I heard you crying in the middle of the night, so I came to check on you. You looked awful. I thought you'd gone mad."

"What have you been doing? Have you been awake?" Shunsuke asked, getting out of bed.

Two

Shunsuke wondered if the Miwa household had been held to-gether by Michiyo. It wasn't because of the inconvenience of having lost her services; nor was it because of her knowledge of his weakness. The thought came to him at times when he felt that he and Tokiko had turned into monsters.

Were their bodies covered with spines in order to inflict pain on each other? But when Shunsuke dwelled on this idea, he got to feeling that there was something ugly and stagnant about Tokiko, there was the smell of old age. Barely able to get herself up in the morning, she sometimes sat in bed for hours.

Shunsuke stood alongside her bed, as if rooted there, gazing at her until she gestured impatiently that he leave her alone. He had stood there because he was filled to bursting with the urge to put his arms around her and embrace her. But he also wanted to ask her when she was going to get up, to say that a housewife without a maid couldn't behave this way.

Concerned but pretending otherwise, Shunsuke left her alone and went to prepare breakfast. From the kitchen he could hear Tokiko getting up, yawning. Is she hinting at something? What now? It was the start of another anxiety-filled day. He wanted to do something, anything, to restore peace in his home, even if it looked silly. Before her affair, he had tended to view Tokiko apprehensively, indignant for being ignored. Tokiko was sometimes sullen, but as long as Shunsuke did not bother her, she was more or less cheerful. She was gloomier now, which left him feeling uncomfortable and nervous.

In the afternoon, Shunsuke saw a faint light in the darkness of Tokiko's face; he decided to make an overture.

"There's a movie Noriko wants to see. We could all see it together."

"I don't want to go to a movie. I've told you so already."

"It's about Hitler," he persisted. "Charlie Chaplin is in it. It's not a love story."

Tokiko did not respond.

"Why don't we go see it?"

Shunsuke could not remember the last time he suggested a movie to Tokiko. How strange; why was that? He told Noriko to hurry, and soon the three of them were on the bus to Ginza.

On the bus, Shunsuke spoke to the female conductor. "Those two over there are with me; they're my wife and my daughter," he said, almost shouting.

"Which two?"

"Those two, over there. They aren't sitting with me, but that is my wife, and that is my daughter." The conductor stared at Shunsuke, then looked at Tokiko and Noriko. Shunsuke was beginning to attract attention, but he shrugged, prepared to his family from anything anyone might say.

୰

"Why were you looking at me like that?" Tokiko said to him when they got off the bus.

"I wasn't looking at you. You just thought I was," Shunsuke replied. He wanted to say: I was trying to see you the way other people see you, because, after all, you're my wife.

"Yes, you were. I can't stand it when you look at me that way. You do it at home, and you do it in public. Why in the world are we going out anyway?"

"We're just seeing a movie."

But there were other reasons. Although Tokiko complained about how he looked at her all the time, Shunsuke knew that the way he viewed Tokiko in public was different from the way he viewed her at home. In fact, he had the strong urge to tell people on the bus: This is my wife who has done something terrible. Yet, if anyone else were to say it, he would attack that person violently.

As they were walking to the cinema, Tokiko stumbled on a small stone, almost losing her balance; she turned toward Shunsuke and chuckled. For a moment, Shunsuke thought that it was he who had stumbled. When he regained his composure, he observed Tokiko more carefully—her torso and her legs, which had looked voluptuous, even sensuous, at the moment she stumbled; he observed how her body moved, revealing her age.

ꝛ

In the middle of the movie, Shunsuke looked at Tokiko, who was seated between him and Noriko, asleep. With her head bent down, she seemed docile and childlike.

"Dad," whispered Noriko, "Mom looks like a ghost. Shouldn't we wake her up?"

"Leave her alone."

Insisting, Noriko shook Tokiko by the shoulder. "Mom, wake up! You look terrible."

"What?" said Tokiko, not entirely awake. When Noriko shook her a second time, Tokiko lifted her head only to lower it again a moment later.

ꝛ

The Chaplin film over, the second feature, *Pension Mimosas*, came on. Seeing foreign actors again fill the screen, Shunsuke felt pain in his gut.

⌐

On the way home, Tokiko was not in a good mood. Shunsuke, remembering a Russian restaurant nearby, suggested they stop to have a bite. George had once invited them there when American friends of his, a foreign correspondent and his wife, were visiting. Shunsuke hadn't gone since Tokiko wasn't interested. For some reason, Shunsuke was thinking about George, which brought the restaurant to mind.

Looking at the menu, Shunsuke said, "It's expensive, so let's just have something simple. We can eat again when we get home." As soon as he said this, he regretted it.

"In that case, let's leave," said Tokiko, upset. "Where else can we go?"

"Well, I'm not sure if you'd like it, but there's a Chinese restaurant in Roppongi. Or we could just go home and eat."

"I don't want to go home," Tokiko snapped. "You don't know a single place, do you?" She seemed on the verge of tears.

"Let's try the Chinese place, then."

"No, that's fine, let's go home. You know, you're no fun."

"Then let's take a taxi. You want to take a taxi, don't you?"

Shunsuke had never enjoyed going out with Tokiko to eat; he didn't feel comfortable being in a restaurant with her. It was the same walking with her. She seemed interested only in antagonizing him. He wanted to take her home as soon as possible, so that he could feel relief. This afternoon, he had taken his wife and daughter out for some enjoyment, but as always he had failed at the crucial moment and now it was too late to do anything.

Telling them to wait, Shunsuke ran to hail a taxi. He felt that he needed to get one before anybody else, overwhelmed by the fear that by failing in this one task he would cause irreversible damage, that things would forever get worse. He had the feeling that Tokiko was pointing at him, telling people who passed by how dull he was.

When they got out of the taxi, Tokiko walked angrily to the front door. "We go out and you drag me back home," she grumbled.

"I can't afford to give you many luxuries, but I don't indulge myself either," said Shunsuke.

"It's the same as always. You tell me that I should listen to you, that you will give the orders, but it's impossible to trust you. You said you'd changed while you were in America, but you haven't changed at all. You still tell me to do things your way, but you can't do anything right yourself. You just make false promises. I won't be fooled anymore."

"I make promises because I think of other people's wishes. The problem is that eventually I have to think of myself, too. You complain that we had to come back home, but when we're out, I work hard to adjust our pace, to keep us together. But the harder I try, the greater the distance between us. Sometimes I think things would be better if you just agreed to do whatever I told you. That would make me feel more confident. Don't you think I'm right?"

As Shunsuke spoke, Noriko escaped into her room.

"What do you want for dinner?" Tokiko asked with a sigh.

"I'm saying it's best to keep the family in harmony. I'm not fussy about the food we eat."

"I see. So you want to eat family harmony?" Tokiko asked. "I've served you nothing but good, nourishing food, and you sit at the table with a sour expression on your face. Why can't you do something for the family? We waste a lot of time doing useless things and talking nonsense." She stamped her foot in mortification. "And days—"

"But you're going to outlive me," interrupted Shunsuke. Although he found himself grinning, he felt lost.

"Ah!" moaned Tokiko, dismissively. "Days fly by while I let myself do meaningless things. You're happy tormenting me like this, but I want it back! Give it back to me!"

"What can I give you back? Your youth? Is that what you want back?" Shunsuke laughed.

"Laugh as much as you like," Tokiko said, throwing a magazine at him.

"Wait, the reason I laughed . . ." Shunsuke began, feeling awkward. He laughed some more to cover his discomfort.

"Yes, I want it back. I'm saying I want you to give me back my youth."

The way Tokiko said "I'm saying" made Shunsuke laugh again, and while laughing, he reflected that Tokiko had undergone cosmetic surgery many times. The last operation had taken place three weeks before his departure for America; it was to erase a deep crease in her cheek. When she returned from the surgery, she had taken off the bandage to show him the result; the crease was gone, but her cheek was badly swollen.

Since then she had her teeth straightened. The dental work made her mouth seem like it belonged to a different person.

"You are still young. But if you're going to demand your youth back, I have to insist on having mine back too, since we've lived together all these years. No matter who you live with, you lose your youth. It's natural. Let's eat," he said.

Hearing this, Tokiko grew even more impatient, her features contorted. "You really enjoy tormenting me, don't you?" she said. "I know how you operate. You hurt me, you make me cry, and then you pretend that nothing's happened, that everything's fine. You say let's eat, or you start flattering me."

"That's not true," Shunsuke said. He placed his hands on her shoulders. "Please, let's not quarrel." As usual when he tried to make up with Tokiko, he spoke tearfully, an octave lower than usual.

Tokiko glared at him, twisting her mouth.

⁓

Late one Sunday morning, Shunsuke was roused by a commotion in the hallway. Leaving his room with deliberate slowness, He found Tokiko furiously scrubbing the floor. Standing behind her, he told her not to overexert herself.

"How can I stand this terrible dust?" Tokiko responded.

"If it needs to be done, we'll all do it. The children and I can help too. Why don't you rest?" Shunsuke said, smiling.

This made Tokiko angrier, and she scrubbed even harder. Her breathing became labored.

"Stop, Tokiko. You'd better rest. Ryoichi! Noriko! Come here!"

When the children came out of their rooms, Shunsuke handed each of them a wet rag. He got down on his knees and started to scrub the floor to show them how to do it.

Tokiko watched this stubbornly. "That's not the way to do it," she said. "It's better if you don't bother because I'll have to do it all over again anyway. Stop. Don't do it!"

"We're not going to let you do it. You think this rag is too wet, don't you? All right, I'll wring it out. But just leave this to us."

"I'll do it, I said!"

This is what depresses me, Shunsuke said to himself.

Everyone scrubbed the floor as if they were in a competition, but after a while Shunsuke and the children gave up. It's better to have a dusty floor than to see her getting so worked up, Shunsuke was about to say, but he checked himself. No doubt that would have made the situation worse.

"Your helping out this one time, it doesn't mean a thing," Tokiko said, giving Shunsuke a look that chilled his heart.

"It's not easy to find a maid who meets our requirements, as you know, and if we all help, we can manage. It won't just be today. We'll help all the time," he said.

"You're just saying that," Tokiko responded, breathing hard as if in pain.

"But you don't know that yet."

"I won't let you fool me. Nothing ever gets done around here unless I do it. I know that."

"That's why—" Shunsuke said, resuming his scrubbing.

"Give that to me!" Tokiko snatched the rag from him.

Shunsuke, standing back, felt that everything he had done, all the care and thought he had mustered, was hopeless. There was something inexplicable about Tokiko, something that had caused George to say that maybe she was crazy.

"Why don't we try to find another maid. Not a middle-aged woman this time. We'll put an ad in the paper again and see how it goes. And this time, I'll do a thorough investigation even if it means going to see her family. Why don't we do that? So please, stop now."

"It's no use. We'll never find anybody good. Every single maid we've had has turned out to be no good. Other families don't have this problem. I don't understand it."

"I don't think that's true. It only seems that way. It's only now that we've had a problem. Anyway, why don't we try again?"

Shunsuke felt he had done what he needed to placate Tokiko. He had been rational and logical, and he felt more confident; he could look at the situation more objectively.

It was agreed that they would place an ad in the newspaper. Tokiko had done this several times before; that was how they found Michiyo. But even after the decision was made, Tokiko did not seem satisfied.

⌒

Shunsuke decided to go back to the doctor he had seen for the pain in his groin. Maybe he could get an injection for his problems.

"Do nerves become thin and fragile, like the tips of branches?" he asked the doctor.

"It's not as bad as that."

"But some nerves do get damaged. Do you think my nerves are especially damaged?"

"Yes, I think so."

The doctor handed Shunsuke a brochure on problems, symptoms, and methods of treatment. The symptoms seemed familiar, but rather than relief, Shunsuke felt contempt.

"I think my wife and I are suffering from some of the problems described here."

"You should bring her in."

Shunsuke responded halfheartedly.

"Yawning and sleeplessness are not only related to hormonal problems," said the doctor.

"Do you think we've damaged each other's nerves? Are we unusual?"

"There are many couples like you. Of course, I don't know what's gone on between you two."

"Are some people more vulnerable than others?"

The doctor proceeded to administer an injection.

Shunsuke remained seated even after the needle was removed. "What happens if damaged nerves are left untreated?" he asked.

The doctor retreated into the next room. "My wife and I are divorced, if you must know," he said.

Shunsuke sat there, dazed.

A young nurse's aide, about seventeen or eighteen, was preparing some medicine for Shunsuke to take with him.

"Do you know anyone who has been cured by this medicine?" he asked her.

"It's very effective. You'll be fine after thirty injections."

"I see," Shunsuke said, frowning like a baby about to cry. He felt a curious affection toward this young nurse, as if she was his mother.

꙳

"Where do I get the injection?" Tokiko asked, exposing her thigh. Shunsuke had secured some medicine for her as well. "Isn't the thigh better than the arm?"

They were sitting in Shunsuke's room, the smallest room in the house. It was soundproofed, so that Shunsuke could have quiet when he was working, although the soundproofing didn't shut out everything. The television one room away could not be heard, but Shunsuke could easily hear Tokiko's moving about in her bedroom, applying her makeup, shutting a book, switching the lamp on or off, yawning.

"Do you really want me to do it? I'm not a doctor, you know," said Shunsuke.

"Go ahead, do it."

As the needle penetrated her skin, Tokiko screamed. Something was wrong, she said.

Shunsuke took off his glasses and examined the needle carefully. The tip was bent a little. "It must have happened after I put it in."

"It hurts so bad. Can you rub it, please," Tokiko said, pulling down her skirt.

Tokiko watched as Shunsuke tried to draw more medicine into the syringe; he was having a hard time because air kept getting in. Even though he couldn't get all of the medicine in, he went ahead and stuck the needle into his thigh. Then he drew more medicine into the syringe and stuck the needle into a different spot on his thigh.

"Why are you so serious about this?" Tokiko said, sighing. "You're just like a kid. You know how Ryoichi pushes and shoves to get a seat when he gets on a bus? You're just like that."

"You're probably right," Shunsuke almost shouted.

⌒

Why hadn't he let Tokiko and George have their affair? Shunsuke was wondering. They'd done it once; what difference would it have made if they kept on? But what would have happened then? As she said, she could have gone somewhere far, very far, away from him.

Then what would she have experienced, how would it have been each time? As she said, she might have felt more fulfillment. Instead of her having halfhearted intercourse with her worn-out, ill-tempered husband, she could have enjoyed it more fully with George.

Shunsuke looked around his room—at the desk, the cushions, the bookshelves, the bed, the splash-patterned kimono. What are these things really? he wondered. Tokiko had helped put the bookshelves up. The desk had been purchased from a man who sold them going from house to house. The same with the plants flowering in the garden: a man came around selling them, and suddenly the plants were in their garden, there were flowers, and they were still there, not dead. That must have been in the spring, and the man with the desk came shortly afterward. Tokiko negotiated the price. And the futon, too. One day Tokiko decided to change the batting, and a few days later a man arrived on a bicycle, carrying a large bundle of cotton.

Standing up, Shunsuke leaned against the door, bracing himself against it with both hands, as though doing push-ups. If I walk out of this room, he thought, I will have to face the family, but if I stay in here, I won't be able to let them know how I feel. He stayed in this posture for a while, thinking how ridiculous he must appear. Then it came to him, he knew what to do. Like a man about to settle an earthshaking matter, he opened the door and dashed out of his room.

In the living room, he found Tokiko and Noriko in front of the television set. Tokiko was dozing; she only seemed to be able to sleep if there was some kind of noise around. Feeling that he was no longer Miwa Shunsuke, but a mere trifle of existence, say, a small rock, he stepped into the room.

"Tokiko."

"What?" she asked, rousing herself.

"Can you come here for a second?"

"What's wrong with here?"

"Well, I want you to come *here*."

Wearily, Tokiko lifted herself up. In the hallway Shunsuke said to her, "I want to put up a fence."

"A fence?"

"To enclose the property."

"A fence," Tokiko murmured a second time, as if groping her way toward the light. "You want to put up a fence?"

"Yes, a tall fence."

"Instead of a fence . . ." Tokiko said, looking down, thinking; color was returning to her face. "Instead of a fence, I think we should move . . . But wait . . ." She seemed lost in thought, having forgotten that Shunsuke was there. "Better yet, we should remodel this house. A fence is a secondary thing."

"I don't agree."

"I know I'm right," Tokiko said, becoming aggressive. "A tall fence won't do what you want it to; you'll regret it later. Knowing you, I'm sure of it. You shouldn't be shortsighted; nothing will happen if we only build a fence." She looked like she was in pain. "But if you have to build a tall fence, we should do something about the house, too."

"Oh, let's just forget it," cried Shunsuke.

⁓

In the middle of that night, Shunsuke opened the door to Tokiko's room and tiptoed to her bed. He lay down next to her and closed his eyes. He did not get under the covers. For a while he remained still. He did not touch her, trying instead to absorb her female scent. With his eyes still closed, he turned toward Tokiko and put his face over hers. When he opened his eyes, he saw that hers were wide open.

They were staring into empty space. She glanced at Shunsuke only to shift her gaze away. When he lay back down, he heard her speak, almost to herself, softly, "Rather than the fence, we should do something about the house. That kitchen was a mistake; you can't call it real kitchen. But if we're going to spend the money on the kitchen, it would—"

"But I was thinking only about the fence. I want to enclose the entire property," he said, studying Tokiko's reaction. What he wanted was to shut Tokiko up in the house, so that she would think only about him and the children, but of course he didn't say so.

"The important thing is the quality of life inside, how we live together in harmony," he said instead. He wasn't sure if Tokiko was listening; her eyes were still fixed somewhere in the air.

"We should move to a new place then," said Tokiko after a while. Shunsuke wondered if she meant no fence was necessary if they moved. "We need a fence for privacy, but I want to move. Let's move." Tokiko's voice was more cheerful now.

"OK," said Shunsuke.

Her coming up with an idea out of blue like this could be detrimental to the family, Shunsuke thought, but, if this kept her engaged and enthusiastic, and if she depended on him for support, then it would be fine. It would make her think about him.

~

Tokiko's being wrapped up in her idea of a new house let Shunsuke forget about the fence. When he saw her gazing vacantly at the garden, however, he grew uneasy. He was afraid she might have given up the idea of moving, so he reminded her of it.

But she hadn't forgotten. "If we're going to have a new house, it has to have central heating, like houses in America," he heard her saying to herself. He was surprised that Tokiko was thinking such a thing.

"How it's done is oil is burned in the basement and heat is sent through ducts to each room. All you need in winter is a blanket," he explained. Tokiko paid no attention to this information he'd acquired from living in America.

"We must also have air-conditioning for summer."

"That way we won't need to go to a resort, and I'll be able to work at home the whole time. We'll all sleep better, too," Shunsuke said. Natural breezes are best, however, he was thinking. Living in the kind of house Tokiko has in mind will be like living in a hotel; it won't feel comfortable. Even if he could manage to finance it, he'd feel uneasy, knowing what his friends and acquaintances would say when they visited.

When he was in America, Shunsuke had stayed for a while at a farm where his host disliked air-conditioning. It was this man's sentiment—that "natural breezes are better"—that Shunsuke remembered well. The farmer had let him use a small, ancient fan, the only fan he owned. When he turned on the switch, the blades started to move after a few seconds, making a primitive whirring sound in the small room of the two-story painted wooden house he was lodged in.

"Let's sell this house and buy a piece of land somewhere," Tokiko said.

"Where should it be?"

"I want you to be in charge this time."

"Of course," Shunsuke answered, feeling a sense of desperation. He wondered what exactly Tokiko had in mind.

ʡ

Responding to the newspaper ad for a maid, Yamane Masako came to the house in a rather stylish yellow dress and a hat. She had a fair complexion, a round cheerful face, and tiny feet, which were swallowed up in the slippers she wore in the house. She was small and slender.

Shunsuke did not say a word when Tokiko described their new maid as a girl with a flat chest who giggles and scurries about like a mouse. She probably has a light menstrual flow, Tokiko added.

"When we move to the new house, I'll let you have a nice room. I'll find you a good husband, too," Tokiko promised Masako. As she had done before with a new maid, she made Masako the present of a couple of blouses.

ﻉ

The Miwas purchased a piece of land about forty minutes from Shinjuku on the Odakyu Line. An architect drew up plans for the house, which was to be built on a slope. It was to have expansive windows, central heating, and central air-conditioning.

"Let's put in a swimming pool, too. The children need exercise, and this will be another way to save money and avoid having to go to the ocean. As you know, I don't like mountains," said Tokiko.

I should keep my objections to myself, Shunsuke thought. He wanted to keep Tokiko happy.

"Where is the bedroom?" he asked, as he inspected the architectural plans.

"My bedroom is downstairs; it's a traditional Japanese-style tatami room. But, actually, I don't like it there," Tokiko responded, frowning.

If this frowning continues, all will be lost, Shunsuke thought.

"Your study can be your bedroom, and when we have a guest, I'll sleep with you," Tokiko continued.

"Then, I'll come down to your bedroom when we don't have guests? Since it's a Japanese-style room, that means we'll have to put a lock on the sliding doors. The children are growing up, after all; they could walk in on us."

"You've changed, you know."

"I want to swim in the pool with you," said Shunsuke, now feeling that this new home could be a paradise.

Shunsuke and Tokiko would swim playfully in the pool, and then, lying on the grass, embrace. He would feel her middle-aged flesh against his, but in this imagined world, they are both young and blossoming. Are we testing our courage? he asks himself. Then, they are in their bedroom. Even though her body is as heavy as his, he holds her as if she is a little child. His rosy yearnings are many times more intense than they were in his youth. We'll have a nice little chat afterwards, he thinks, and say nothing about the future, which would make them feel lonely. They will talk quietly about the past, about the time before they met. Or they will gossip about other people's problems . . .

ع

"Feel right here. Here . . . Don't you feel it?" asked Tokiko, pushing Shunsuke away. He had been holding her and pressing his lips to her upper arm.

"Here? Is this it?"

"Ouch!" she exclaimed, grimacing. She thrust her breasts toward Shunsuke.

"Your breasts are so fine, so full," he said, caressing them.

"My left breast bothered me when I stopped nursing, and now it gets sore when I have my period. Here, right here," she said, putting his hand to the spot. Her eyes gleamed.

"It isn't the same as when it gets full just before your period?"

"You feel it, don't you?"

"When did you first notice this?" Shunsuke asked, thinking that Tokiko was acting like she had discovered buried treasure.

"I'm not sure. Noriko heard about it at school, and she told me. So I examined myself and found it. Lumps are the size of a bean usually, and they don't necessarily hurt."

"Where did you learn that?"

Tokiko pointed to a magazine on top of her dresser. Shunsuke read the article, but it was so vague that he couldn't tell if the lump Tokiko had discovered really suggested the possibility of the dread disease.

"It's not possible that I have cancer. No one in my family had cancer, and I am healthy. My monthly flow is always full, much heavier than any maid's we've had.

"You're right. I'm sure you're fine," said Shunsuke eagerly.

↵

The Miwas moved from their old house. Because construction of their new house was taking longer than they had anticipated, they took up temporary residence in what had once been a company dormitory in T City. They moved their belongings in three trucks; their dog barked the whole time, trembling in Ryoichi's arms.

↵

In the lobby at the hospital, Tokiko and Shunsuke sat close together, waiting for her turn. The patient next to them was filling out a form, which Shunsuke glanced at. His heart started to race. There was a question about "caressing," and the patient was to choose from "sufficient," "adequate," and "insufficient." Tokiko must have filled out the same form when she'd come to see the doctor by herself earlier. How had she responded?

↵

Shunsuke waited for Tokiko outside the examination room. Her doctor emerged and came up to him. "It is cancer, but you must know that already," the doctor said.
"No, I didn't know."
"I'm afraid we're going to need to remove a large part of her breast."

↵

After three hours, Tokiko was wheeled out of surgery and left in front of him like a heavy log. Shunsuke was unnerved but helped the nurse tidy her up. He is her husband, that's why he is here beside her like this, there's no doubt that they are husband and wife, he said to himself, as if he was a third person watching this happen. Tokiko had often complained that he chose to look away at crucial moments in life. Now, slowly, her vacant eyes were achieving a focus, and she looked right into his eyes.

"The doctor says you're going to be fine."

"What does he mean by 'fine'?"

"They got everything out, so you don't have to worry."

"I didn't have cancer."

"I know that. It was something else of a malignant nature, but the doctor had to give that diagnosis in order to secure a bed for you. They fight over empty beds among themselves, you know," he said.

A different doctor, not the one he had spoken to earlier, called Shunsuke out of the room. "The tumor had grown quite large, and it was surrounded by fatty tissue. Is it true that your wife came here alone for her first visit?"

"Yes."

"Surely you understand that we don't give the patient the full diagnosis. Usually, it's the husband who finds out the truth, and he keeps it a secret from his wife and family. Where were you when your wife came here, may I ask?"

"I was working. I couldn't get away. We . . . I have to work hard. We're in the middle of having a house built, and the money . . ."

"But the house is less important, isn't it? After all, it's not like you don't have a place to live. I've also had a house built, but from what I can see, your feet are not firmly on the ground. I've operated on your wife's breast, and although you didn't ask me directly—and I am not the head of the department—I'm saying you should not have let her come by herself earlier. Did she insist on coming without you?"

"Yes, she did," Shunsuke replied. It seemed certain that the doctor hadn't received the gift he sent him through the hospital.

"You really should not have let that happen, Mr. Miwa. You have to be more supportive. Furthermore, why did you let it go for so long? You must have known about her lump for three months. I've never heard of something like this happening among well-educated people like you. It's not so hard to detect breast cancer, since you can feel it externally. What were you doing these three months? Haven't you talked about it between yourselves?"

"She'd gone to a clinic a few times before she came here. She was convinced it was mastitis."

"You didn't go with her to the clinic either?"

"No, I didn't."

"You are not like most people," the doctor said, sounding angry.

"What are the chances of recurrence?"

"I removed the entire tumor, so I don't think you have to worry too much. But you have to be sure she gets good follow-up attention. There is no guarantee. After all, the operation was rather late," the doctor said, wanting to make sure Shunsuke understood the situation.

～

Shunsuke had been staying at the hospital, spending nights on a rented mattress, which he spread out on a board kept under Tokiko's bed.

"Honey," Tokiko called out to Shunsuke, who was lying down even though it was daytime. "Can you massage me here? My arm is numb."

"That's because of the bandage. It needs to be tight to help the healing."

"I know that. I don't need to hear it from you. But can't you do something? I've got powerful lungs, and tying them down so hard hurts."

Shunsuke got up and began massaging her. An hour passed, but Tokiko did not ask him to stop. Out of the corner of his eyes, he watched her open her eyes occasionally and glance at him. They would quiver faintly, as though they were deflating.

"What are we doing here?"

"You're rubbing my arm, and I'm glaring at you."

"You aren't glaring."

"Honey—"

"What?"

"I want to take a bath."

Shunsuke nodded, continuing his massage.

"Can you wash my feet, please? You know, I'm embarrassed when I think how I must have looked on the operating table, like some Indian woman, with my clothes slipping off."

Shunsuke took time to rearrange her hospital gown. He kissed her on her stomach.

Tokiko was quiet. Shunsuke wondered what she was thinking.

"I have no desire for anything right now, but in three weeks, I want to have a long bath," she said as Shunsuke covered her with a blanket.

"Don't worry about anything," he said.

"I don't want to go to the neighborhood public bath. Not looking like this. You'll have to see that our new house gets finished soon. It was your idea after all."

"Construction workers are so lazy."

As they talked, the door opened, and Ryoichi walked in. He seemed to be sulking.

"Can you stay for a couple hours?" Shunsuke asked his son. "I need to grab something to eat. Then I have to meet someone about work, and I want to go for a walk."

"OK, but be sure to come back in two hours."

"Of course. I'll see you then," Shunsuke said.

Ryoichi looked skeptical.

After having a bowl of noodles, Shunsuke went to a grocery store and, surrounded by housewives, spoke to the clerk. "I'd like some oranges and apples, the best ones you have, please," he said.

"Yes, sir, the best oranges and the best apples for you."

With the fruit in a bag made from pages of a magazine, Shunsuke stopped at another store, this one where Western-style bathtubs were sold. It was a clear day, and the sun cast a soft light on the tubs displayed in the window.

"Does this tub get dirty easily?" he asked the clerk.

"To a degree, yes, but it keeps the water temperature remarkably well."

"In this model, both hot and cold water come out through the same faucet. Won't the water reverse itself under high pressure?"

"No, it won't because there's a device to prevent that from happening. Are you thinking of buying this model?"

"Yes, but I don't know when."

"Where do you live?"

"In T City on the Odakyu Line."

"That's a nice area, isn't it?"

"Nothing special."

"What kind of tub do you have now?"

"Now? We don't have any. We're living in temporary quarters. But this tub looks small even for one person."

"It's big enough. It's not meant for two people, though."

"That's not what I had in mind. I just don't want to find out afterward it was wrong for us."

"I understand."

"No, you don't," Shunsuke snapped. He had become irritated with the salesclerk all of a sudden.

"Do you enjoy soaking in a bath?"

"Not especially."

"Does your wife?"

"My wife? We don't like it particularly. We don't bathe because we enjoy it."

༈

When Shunsuke returned to the hospital room, Ryoichi was sitting with his head buried in his arms: neither a child nor an adult.

"After you left, they gave me a blood transfusion for at least an hour, and then they gave me more injections," Tokiko said.

"I'm going now," said Ryoichi, who got his things and left.

"Honey—"

"What is it, dear?"

"That nurse's expression changed the moment she saw Ryoichi."

༈

Shunsuke stopped sleeping at the hospital from the second week on; he visited often but did not stay very long. When he couldn't go, Ryoichi did.

"Mom said you leave as soon as someone comes to visit, as if you're waiting for the chance. She told me to tell you that," Ryoichi said to Shunsuke one day.

"Did she really?"

"She also said she was ready to come home but first she wants to soak in the bathtub in that other room."

"You mean the private room that costs five thousand yen a day."

"She said there're even better rooms. Oh, and she also asked if you could bring . . . what you call those things . . . ?"

Those things . . . those things for her period, thought Shunsuke.

༈

When he went to the hospital the next day, Shunsuke inquired into the private room with a bath and learned that it was available.

When he got to Tokiko's room, she moved her head and looked at him with a dissatisfied expression, ready to complain.

"The private room with a bath is on the third floor," Shunsuke said.

Observing him carefully, she remained silent.

"I wonder what kind of tub it has," he continued.

"I have no idea."

"How about moving to that room? It's available now."

"I don't think the rooms here are anything special. I don't want to bathe in a tub that someone else has used. Until we have our own tub, I'm not soaking in anybody's," she said. And then she added, "You ought to be ashamed of yourself, making your son deliver those things." Those things for her period.

～

Having packed the suitcase, husband and wife got in a taxi, leaving the hospital for home. Tokiko was half-lying down most of the way, sleeping against Shunsuke.

Shunsuke talked to himself, but the voice he heard was Michiyo's.

"I've heard, Madam, that Caucasian men are passionate lovers, and they try very hard to satisfy their women. They're not like Japanese men at all. Do you know that they talk to you afterward too? Maybe some Japanese men will talk to you, but not after it's over. They tell the woman about going to an exotic island in a yacht, staying all by themselves, or about going out to a sumptuous dinner. Things like that. Not just middle-aged men, mind you, young men are like that, too. Talk about having no style . . ."

Why did Tokiko get this illness? Shunsuke wondered. Why did the affair with George happen? Was there a connection between the two? Was he, Shunsuke, responsible?

The taxi was approaching the street of their old house when Shunsuke realized his error and called out to the driver, "Stop! Pull over here."

Tokiko woke up and looked out the window. "What's the matter?" she asked.

"This isn't the right place, driver. We want T City."

Shunsuke had not only given the driver the address of their old house but he had also been directing him to it. At the site of their old house there was nothing but bare land enclosed by a low fence. Their old house had been demolished.

"I asked what's the matter," Tokiko said.

Tokiko should have left me when she was younger, Shunsuke thought. In fact, it would have been better if she never married me.

࿐

Shunsuke was passing Ryoichi's room one afternoon when he saw, through the crack of the open door, his son embracing Masako, the young maid. He tiptoed away and went upstairs to Tokiko.

"Go peek into Ryoichi's room," he said to his wife, who seemed cheerful. He then walked away, without saying anything more, through the hall down the stairs.

From the kitchen, he could hear Tokiko's voice: "What are you two doing? Come out of there!" Shunsuke busied himself as if he needed something; he turned on the water faucet and drank directly from it. He could hear Ryoichi coming down the stairs and putting on his shoes to go out. He left without saying a word.

࿐

"Where is he?" Tokiko asked.

"Out, it seems," Shunsuke answered.

"Oh," Tokiko said calmly. "I asked Masako why she let him do it, and she said she loved Ryoichi. It wasn't anything frivolous, she said."

"I wonder when this got started."

"I told Masako that if something happens to her, I wouldn't know how to apologize to her parents. Open your eyes and see what Ryoichi is after, I told her. If he was serious at all, he would be standing here with you now, I said. Knowing you'd be questioned, he'd try to protect you, not leave the house. I'm his mother, so I know. He's not a responsible type, but if I told him that, he'd say that this wasn't anything serious and that he's not a fool. I told Masako this, and what do you think she said? She smiled and said, 'I know him better than you do.'" Tokiko started laughing, which startled Shunsuke.

Tokiko then said that she told Masako to move out.

"In my own house, I won't have it," she continued, indignant. "Imagine, that flat-chested girl talking about love! You better get her out tomorrow. I don't want her making demands on Ryoichi later on."

Shunsuke nodded gravely.

⁓

The next morning, Shunsuke put Masako and her bags in the same taxi that he was taking Tokiko to the local hospital in. Tokiko had been undergoing a course of radiation therapy. When Tokiko got out at the hospital, Masako stole a nervous look at her, but Tokiko ignored her. Masako sobbed, then all of the sudden she stopped.

Shunsuke dropped her off at the nearest train station, checking her luggage in to her parents' rural address; he bid her good-bye. Masako was wearing a casual dress, not like the stylish one she wore on her first day. She looked at him reproachfully.

⁓

"Until our house gets done and we're settled in, you can expect anything to happen," said Tokiko at home that afternoon.

⌐

Masako came by to the Miwa household the next day. Shunsuke was relieved to see her but did not say so.

"I don't think I did anything wrong," Masako said, "but I'm very fond of Mrs. Miwa, so I'd like to stay if you let me. As I was told, I will think only of my future."

"I was only thinking of your own good," Tokiko said. She turned to Shunsuke and asked, "What do you think, honey?"

"I thought from the start it was Ryoichi's fault," he said.

"I want to take sewing lessons," Masako said.

Without openly admitting it, Shunsuke, as well as Tokiko, knew that they couldn't do without Masako.

So Masako was their maid again. When Ryoichi returned home that afternoon, Masako ignored him.

⌐

In April the Miwas moved into their new house. They were greeted with all kinds of new noises—from the two lavatories, the garbage disposal, the gas water heater. Moreover, when the flush of the toilet wouldn't stop for some reason, there was the sound of something being dragged around, as well as the gasping of the motor in the septic tank. When it rained, leaks from the veranda appeared in several places in the living room. Seeing the water dripping into her bedroom, Tokiko screamed as if a fire had broken out. Repairmen were summoned, but as they could not correct the original problem, it leaked every time it rained.

⌐

Naked and upset, Tokiko walked out of the bathroom, where a pink Western-style bathtub and matching pink toilet had been installed. She walked into her bedroom and stood in front of the mirror, examining the breast that had been operated on. She called Shunsuke, who was on the veranda, doing household chores. Whenever he had time, he had been filling cracks in the wall or making flower boxes.

"Can you feel this here, honey?"

"Where? Is it here?"

"Do you feel something hard there?"

Shunsuke felt a spot, at the muscle near where most of the flesh had been cut away, somewhat swollen.

"The radiation they're giving me isn't working. Their machine is old. And, you know, we made a big mistake moving here. I wish we still lived in the middle of Tokyo. Besides, look at this house! It's the biggest mistake we've ever made. Ah—what are you thinking?" Tokiko sighed.

"Well, I'm thinking about the house. We can't blame everything on the architect and the contractor. No matter what our problems are, we have to make this house comfortable to live in. I have to think about money, too."

ل

One day Shunsuke came home to find Tokiko in bed with her hand on her breast.

"They cut my breast again," she said, staring at him. "Don't look away."

Shunsuke managed a faint smile.

Tokiko asked him to come to her. "This is where they cut! Here!" She showed him the spot in the same way she might teach a young child where breasts are. She then shifted her body and pulled his hand to her intact breast with a force that surprised him.

"Take it easy. You've just had a surgery," Shunsuke said.

~

It was summer. Shunsuke returned home one day to find Tokiko and Ryoichi talking and laughing with Michiyo in the living room. Michiyo was visiting with her ten-year-old son, who had always been fond of Ryoichi. Shunsuke sat down with them in the living room, missing the chance to excuse himself. Both Tokiko and Shunsuke had known that Ryoichi had been visiting Michiyo occasionally, but they had not said anything about it to him. If they had objected, they would have to admit to each other that they were still upset about the incident, and Ryoichi would sense that something was wrong; he would ask questions. He was no longer willing to accept things without explanation.

"Congratulations! This is such a fine house," Michiyo, who looked heavier, said to Shunsuke. Tokiko stayed calm, as if nothing was the matter. Michiyo then complained about her small apartment, that it wasn't easy since she got arthritis and gained weight. Since she couldn't work because of her arthritis, she would gain even more weight, she said. "Even if you wanted me to, Mrs. Miwa, I couldn't work for you now."

"We have Masako," Tokiko replied.

As Shunsuke listened to the conversation, smiling but saying nothing, he wondered to himself if it was possible to bring Michiyo back to work for them.

"I want to show this house to George," Ryoichi piped up. He then went on to explain that George was now discharged from the military, and had gone into the import-export business with some money he inherited unexpectedly. He was doing well, Ryoichi said.

"That's what I was saying. You must show him this Western-style house with a veranda full of flowers," said Michiyo, looking up at Shunsuke in her usual unflinching way.

"George must be making a lot of money then. He's really wonderful," remarked Tokiko with her eyes on Shunsuke. "I hope my husband makes a lot of money, since we had to borrow a lot to build this house. Just maintaining it is pretty expensive. So, my husband, you're going to have to work hard, aren't you?"

Tokiko did not say anything about her illness.

"George is probably too busy to come to see us. Besides, this flimsy house is a poor example of Japanese culture. It only looks halfway decent with flowers and plants around," said Shunsuke.

"I wish we had a swimming pool," said Ryoichi petulantly.

"I won't let him say no," said Tokiko. "George has got to come see us and congratulate us on our house. After all we've done for him . . ."

"Then we should invite him for dinner," said Shunsuke.

"I'll bring him. I can call him or go to his house," Ryoichi volunteered.

"Don't forget to tell him your father says hello," Tokiko said.

Just what Tokiko had meant by this was not clear to Shunsuke, but for some time now he had adopted the attitude that to humor her was best. She was acting casual, so it was best for him to do the same. If he showed antagonism toward George, Michiyo would think he and Tokiko were not getting along. If George did come to visit, he should be received without a fuss. The incident was not that serious after all. In a way, it was he and Tokiko who should apologize to George. But if an invitation is going to be extended, George has got to accept it, thought Shunsuke. Not knowing exactly why, he felt it was important, that he had to make sure George would come. If he didn't, he thought, Tokiko would lose confidence in herself. Tokiko, who has lost a breast. It would have been nice if they had a swimming pool.

Shunsuke started to feel that life was worth living. Was it because of his excitement about the fact that this man whom he had hated was going to show up in his house? Certainly, that was a part of it, but there was something else—it was a kind of empathy on his part. Realizing that other people were trying hard to live their lives, that it wasn't just himself, he felt an unexpected closeness to George.

⁓

Later that day, Shunsuke took his children and Michiyo's son to a community swimming pool.

Noriko, seeing her father swim, laughed and said he had the most rigid stroke of everyone in the entire pool.

Tokiko was in an especially good mood that night, and she startled Shunsuke by poking him in the chest when they passed each other in the hallway.

"How are you, my handsome husband?" she said.

When Shunsuke didn't know how to respond, she teased him more. "I haven't seen you in my room lately. Isn't it about time you came by to see me?" she said, winking. Then she imitated his frown, which might have been her way of showing affection. "Don't worry, I won't demand that you come. But you're too serious, you know. At times like this you should laugh and pay no attention to me."

"Hmm." Shunsuke forced a smile.

"Show that you're confident and act like the man of the house," Tokiko went on as she patted him on the lower back.

I like Tokiko when she acts like this, Shunsuke said to himself. He grabbed her and gave her a kiss.

Tokiko, who didn't like to be kissed, turned her face away. How did she manage George's kisses? Shunsuke wondered. Did she enjoy them?

"I won't let George despise us Japanese," Tokiko said abruptly, "just because of that thing that happened."

Shunsuke thought Tokiko might be right, and thinking of what she had just said, he was suddenly close to tears.

"What do you think about asking Michiyo to come back?" he said after a bit.

"No, she's no good. A woman with arthritis can't do any work."

"Maybe you're right."

*

"She's your former maid, Madam? Such a talker, isn't she?" said Masako.

"Her mouth moves faster than her hands," Tokiko responded spitefully.

*

Ryochi returned with the news that, yes, George would come to visit. Ryoichi was going to call George to arrange the date, and he asked his father to talk with George. Shunsuke knew he had to do this in order to make George feel welcome.

Shunsuke talked in a gentle voice, saying that he was happy George had returned to Tokyo, that he was sorry about what had happened between them, and that Michiyo had come to visit them with her son. It was too bad that it was summer, as the view from the house was particularly good in fall and winter, he added. This was to make George, thus Tokiko, feel comfortable, he said to himself. George said that Japan and America should try to get along. These words angered Shunsuke, but he controlled himself. "That's right. I think so," he said. "I think so."

"You didn't mention your mother's illness to him, did you?" Shunsuke asked Ryoichi. He said it in an offhanded manner so that he could excuse himself in case Tokiko wanted to know why he had asked such a question.

"Of course not," Ryoichi replied with rare decisiveness.

*

On the morning of the day of George's visit, Shunsuke turned on the air-conditioner. If it is cool out , the effect will be lost, he thought, but a hot day with nice breezes would be worse yet because with the doors open, no air conditioning would be needed at all.

He then went out to the garden to pull weeds. For this day, he had specially ordered a blind to hang outside the big picture window. Though the veranda was quite wide, the glare of the sun invaded the upper floor on a hot day. The blind was not cheap.

Shunsuke watered the flowers in the planters on the veranda. With meager nourishment from the soil in the pots, the salvia, cockscomb, and other flowers were barely surviving. On some days, these flowers were a source of irritation, and on others they brought satisfaction. When they seemed legitimately cheerful, he felt happiness, but when they suggested falseness, a facade, he was resentful.

"Have you turned on the air-conditioner? It's not cool in here at all," Tokiko said when she came in from the veranda.

"It's on. Everything doesn't get cool right away," Shunsuke replied, but he went down to the basement to check anyway, to prevent Tokiko from falling into a bad mood. He could tell, however, even before he opened the basement door, that the motor wasn't working. The fan was broken.

"I knew something was wrong. What should we do? Do something. Why does this have to happen on the very day we need it most," cried Tokiko.

Shunsuke stood there, helpless.

"Why don't we call an electrician and tell him to come at once?" Tokiko suggested.

"Calm down," said Shunsuke.

"How can I? It'll look so bad if . . ."

Shunsuke tried to compose himself. He must not make Tokiko angry, because if he does, everything will go down the drain, all of the effort he put in since the affair, all of the hard work he put into the house . . . If that happened, he wouldn't know how he could go on living.

ↄ

The electrician determined that dust had caused overheating. "The motor needs oil, too. Haven't you oiled it at all? And the filter's full of dust. You can't expect it to work like this."

"Please fix it immediately. We're having an important guest," Tokiko demanded, almost hysterical.

She then turned to Shunsuke and told him to see that the problem was solved; she had to go to a beauty parlor. Also, as it was Masako's day off, she had to attend to tasks in the kitchen.

Then she summoned her son. "Ryoichi," she said, "be sure you meet George at the curb."

"Why are you making such a fuss, Mom?" Noriko piped up. "It's only that American who's coming. He said something bad about you, didn't he?"

"Please stop that talk," Shunsuke intervened before Tokiko could respond; he wanted to spare her any embarrassment.

ↄ

Ryoichi ushered George through the garden. He walked him around the lotus pond, looking triumphant. Shunsuke was about to put his arm around Tokiko's waist as they came into the house, but he stopped himself.

"You've gained some weight, haven't you? And you have a beard!" Tokiko laughed, pointing at George's face.

Before George could reply, Shunsuke said how becoming the beard was.

George entered the living room with a serious look on his face and made an exaggerated gesture of surprise. The house, he said, was like a summer villa in California, which Ryoichi translated for his mother right away.

Today I will just smile and be helpful, Shunsuke said to himself; let Ryoichi do the translating. I will retire to my room, and later, I will come back and join everyone before returning to work again.

After showing George around the house, Ryoichi took him out on the veranda to let him see the view from there. The plan was to put a pool over there, it'll get done some day, Shunsuke heard his son saying.

Shunsuke thought he should help Tokiko and Noriko in the kitchen and went downstairs.

"He's got a bad smell. I can still remember the smell on the sheets he slept on," Noriko said.

"He's grown up quite a bit," said Tokiko to no one in particular.

"It was disgusting," Noriko went on.

"I'll talk with him a little, about his work, just to get the conversation going. You should let Ryoichi do the entertaining," said Shunsuke.

"Why do you have to say things like that?" Tokiko said.

"He must feel awkward, and also I think it'll be better for you."

"Why do you think so?"

"Well, it's important that I look like the head of the household, isn't it?" Shunsuke regretted saying this the instant it came out of his mouth. He hadn't meant to say anything meaningful, but whenever he opened his mouth, he sounded like he was explaining himself.

"Do whatever you want. I don't care."

"Dad, you should stay here."

"You're so unreliable. You're not thinking of my illness, either."

"Oh, all right then. I'll stay," Shunsuke said immediately.

༄

During dinner, George talked about his work and his impressions of Tokyo, seeming quite solemn. Shunsuke noticed that George was directing most of his attention to him.

"I'll go to my room after all," Shunsuke whispered to Tokiko, signaling Noriko with his eyes. When Tokiko didn't say anything, he told George that he had to excuse himself and get back to work; he nodded in George's direction and then smiled at him. As he climbed the stairs, he heard laughter at the table.

～

An hour later, Shunsuke came back downstairs.

"Hey, Dad," Ryoichi said, "George could have gotten a used American air-conditioner for less than a fifth of what you paid. He says it would've been more efficient, too."

"It's late. Why don't we ask George to spend the night," Shunsuke said.

Ryoichi persuaded George to stay. George showered and then went upstairs to Shunsuke's room, where he'd be sleeping. Directly below, in Tokiko's room, Shunsuke spread out his bedding next to Tokiko's.

"You didn't have to ask him to stay over," said Tokiko, sitting in front of her mirror.

"I wish you'd told me that earlier," Shunsuke said. Then, suddenly feeling malicious, he added, "If you want, you can go upstairs to him. I don't mind."

"Then why don't you get out of here?"

"Fine."

Shunsuke carried his bedding to the maid's room. He lay down with the light on and his eyes open. He could hear Tokiko's opening and closing her dresser drawers, opening and closing the closet doors, going in and out of the bathroom. She would never cry at a time like this, he said to himself.

Ryoichi, hearing them, came downstairs. "What's the matter with you two, making all this noise?" he said to Tokiko. "Why don't you behave like a decent couple." Then, seeing that Shunsuke was in the maid's room, he said, "Why is Dad sleeping in the maid's room?"

He walked to where Shunsuke was lying in bed.

"Mom doesn't want George to find out about her illness, does she? If you two carry on like this, he'll suspect something."

"Could you take care of your mother tonight, please?" Shunsuke whispered. He went on, suddenly feeling gentle toward his son, "I know you've done a lot today, and I appreciate it."

"Ryoichi, come here and rub my back," Tokiko was calling out from her room. Nearly in tears, Ryoichi went to his mother.

　　　　　　　　　　　　　ᶜ

After he had spent some time with her, Ryochi came back to his father. "She's tired, and she looks awful," he said. "Why don't you go to her?"

Shunsuke found Tokiko lying on her side, facing away from him. Suddenly, she turned her around and glared at him. His first reaction was to run, but instead he sat down beside her and touched her shoulder. He began massaging her back while she wriggled, trying to get away from him.

"What a rotten son I have. He can't even rub my back," she sobbed. Shunsuke felt relieved. He continued massaging her until near daybreak.

　　　　　　　　　　　　　ᶜ

George was up at eight, but Tokiko was unable to leave her bed and the children slept late. Shunsuke and George had breakfast alone. Shunsuke said that Tokiko had a stomachache. George seemed uncomfortable. He sighed and kept looking out the window at young women on their way to work.

　　　　　　　　　　　　　ᶜ

In autumn, it was decided that Tokiko needed to have another operation.

Tokiko and Shunsuke rode in a taxi that drove slowly under trees in full foliage. Traffic was so congested near Shinjuku that the car could barely move, making Tokiko furious.

They were in the office of Dr. K, who had examined Tokiko and confirmed a metastasis in her lung. He stated this in front of Tokiko rather matter-of-factly.

"We'll give her some male hormone; it comes from Germany. That should help considerably. Then we will surgically remove the tumor. We could also try other medication."

"How does one get this illness, Dr. K?" Shunsuke asked, even though Tokiko was in the same room.

What Shunsuke meant by this question and what the doctor understood it to mean seemed to be at odds, and the doctor responded in a way that had little to do with Tokiko's condition: "Here is a book translated from the French, it's quite interesting. It says that the further our lives are removed from nature, the greater the risk of getting the disease. For example, the risk is smaller if we eat fish than if we eat beef; fish move around a great deal while cows eat grass in a confined area. That's the statistical conclusion. But the truth of the matter is, we don't know much about the cause."

Dr. K took out a crumpled paper and laid it on the desk. "Here are the results of an experiment with mice, showing that the combination of medication and injections of male hormone produced a favorable result. This group here all died while this other group had some survivors. We're conducting more specific research, but it's not enough. We don't have funding. I'm doing some experiments, although our ability to make the serum is limited." He turned to Tokiko. "Well, Mrs. Miwa," he said, "you'll just have to be patient and keep the will to live."

Tokiko seemed taken aback.

"Don't look like that," Dr. K said to her. "You'll be hospitalized soon, but you won't miss your husband too much, I hope. Some patients do, and they don't let their husbands leave, or insist on going home."

Shunsuke was thinking about what the doctor had said earlier: "Sexual desire will increase after the male hormone is injected, and then there'll be some physical changes, male characteristics such as body hair. Your wife is at the age when that sort of thing shouldn't bother her." The doctor had smiled.

When Dr. K stood up, Shunsuke helped Tokiko out of the office. He had a few moments alone with the doctor, during which he said, "My wife and I hadn't been getting along too well. Do you think that could have caused this? I can give you some details if . . ."

"Well, let's try these injections. You can do it at home, so be sure to do it," said the doctor, raising his voice. "In fact, you should be the one to give her the injections. It's best that the husband does it."

Shunsuke blushed at having mentioned "details."

"I hear you've built a rather unusual house," the doctor said, changing the subject. He must have heard about it from Shimizu, a family friend who had recommended this doctor. Shunsuke blushed even more.

౨

Tokiko purchased an alarm clock at the department store, and then she wanted to eat something. By the time they left the restaurant she was exhausted.

"What I've got is asthma. That's what it is," Tokiko said in the taxi on their way home.

Shunsuke thought she might be right. He said he would see Dr. K again to find out more.

A few days later, after having arranged for a check and a gift of canned goods to be delivered to Dr. K, Shunsuke went to see him, bringing along the X-rays that had been taken six months earlier.

"Isn't this just a shadow?" Shunsuke asked anxiously, pointing to a spot on the film.

Dr. K studied the X-ray and frowned. "We should be able to extend your wife's life considerably," he said to Shunsuke.

"Extend . . . ?"

"Yes, a year, three years, twenty years . . . Extend. Try to see things that way. We try to extend life as long as possible. Most illnesses can't be completely cured, you understand. Diabetes, for example. You and I, too, we're extending our lives, aren't we? Mr. Miwa, is there anything else you want to ask?"

Shunsuke didn't have the courage to ask how long Tokiko's life could be extended.

When he returned home, he went straight to Tokiko, who was upstairs in his bed. She was awake, her eyes glaring, her complexion a little darker.

"How did it go?"

"The prognosis was that even with the metastasis, modern medicine can keep you alive for many years. Dr. K seems to be very competent. I think we can have confidence in him."

"And to think that all this time I've been so vain. It's so sad."

"You mustn't think like that," Shunsuke said with a strained smile. He put his hands on her back, beginning to massage her.

Had Tokiko ever mentioned vanity before? If she had, he would have felt differently, less heavyhearted about themselves. But hearing her use the word now, he was shaken. It pained him to see her weakened like this.

After Tokiko fell asleep, Shunsuke went down to the living room, a room designed to be the central gathering place for the family. He sat there alone, and for the first time in the many years of his life with Tokiko, he wept. That was when he noticed a small pool of water on the table before him. He stared at it just as there was a drop from above, which made a splash. It was not raining, but it had rained the day before, so water must have gotten in and been accumulating in a spot above the ceiling.

In the garden, flowers were blooming. The gardener had planted shrubs, which had gone uncared for; on the overgrown branches were many small flowers. The shrubs will die unless measures are taken, Shunsuke thought. But he must not think this way. After the potted flowers on the veranda died, they bought two pots of primroses, a rubber plant, and a bird of paradise. The rubber plant and bird of paradise died when Shunsuke forgot to move them indoors one cold day. The primroses were now outside the window of Tokiko's room.

Beyond the flowers in the garden, Shunsuke could see the family dog pacing restlessly by the fence; occasionally the dog would lie down, keeping his eyes on the house.

At times Tokiko and Shunsuke gazed at the dog together. The dog, a male, had grown quite old. In dog years he was older than Shunsuke, but he still got excited by female dogs; not knowing what to do, he would look at them with pleading eyes, barking.

"How come this old dog is still so active?" Tokiko had asked.

"He sure is. I don't know why."

"Look at his white hair. The hair around his eyes is all white."

As he had done before, the dog with white hair around his eyes watched their every move through the window. Shunsuke stood up and closed the curtain.

~

The male hormone, which Shunsuke injected into Tokiko every three days, gradually darkened her complexion, and her facial hair thickened.

"I still have my periods. I knew they wouldn't stop."

But this one might be her last.

Tokiko's eyes, which were turned toward him as she lay flat on her back in bed, were moist.

"When I look at those cheap magazines, I'm always drawn to the most lurid pictures, you know."

"It won't be good for you. You'll have pain afterward," Shunsuke said to her, but Tokiko held his hand and wouldn't let go of it.

Noriko came to their bed just then, and Shunsuke knew he had to ask her to leave.

"Why do I have to leave?" Noriko complained.

"Never mind and go downstairs. I'll tell you why when you grow up."

He meant what he had said; he thought in all honesty that he would tell his daughter about it when she was older.

Shunsuke lay over Tokiko, bearing his weight on his arms so he would not put pressure on her body. Her facial hair was rough against his well shaven chin. His pubic hair was crushed against hers. Her lower abdomen protruded, which she seemed to find intolerable.

Shunsuke had never seen Tokiko longing so desperately to be loved. Her entire body was appealing to him gently, almost begging. Usually, Tokiko responded to Shunsuke passively or, on occasions when she initiated the contact, aggressively and obligingly. But she was different now. The experience gave Shunsuke a whole new understanding. Everything they owned—the new house, the television set, the stainless steel kitchen sink, the Western-style bathtub, the contemplated swimming pool—as well as the countless hours spent writing and filling out forms, everything, including the salvias and the water lilies, all was for this satisfaction, for what he was experiencing.

"I didn't know it could be like this . . ." Tokiko uttered, words that she must have picked up in the cheap magazine.

Tokiko had not been satisfied by George; when George said "nothing happened," he probably meant that there hadn't been this kind of satisfaction.

Tokiko's bit his tongue, and her teeth ground against his. Her cheeks, which were no longer soft and fair, were hollow, the effect of the facelift long gone; they rubbed against his. When he finally opened his eyes, Shunsuke saw, right in front of him, her graying hair, coarsened even more. There were beads of sweat on her forehead.

What is the nature of this satisfaction? Shunsuke wondered. Is it carnal? No, it's something more. I have finally overcome my inability. I have learned that it was Tokiko who could not respond to lovemaking. It was not me but you, Tokiko, who had problems, he said to himself.

"Is it like this with everybody?" Tokiko asked between moans. "Harder, please."

"It's not good for you . . . Besides, it's not easy in a bed . . . for us Japanese."

Shunsuke meant to say that Japanese were not used to a Western-style bed. But George might have despised the Japanese body—might have been disappointed, felt cheated, by Tokiko's unresponsive body.

Tokiko and I are doing something destined to bear no fruit, Shunsuke thought now.

"Are you all right? Does your chest hurt?" asked Shunsuke.

Tokiko murmured something with her eyes closed. She might have said, "Honey, oh, honey," but it was not clear.

Then, whether from pleasure or from shortness of breath, Tokiko began to gasp for air.

Shunsuke rushed out to get the neighborhood doctor.

He ran through the uneven road filled with the light of the June sun.

As he ran, it occurred to him the words that Tokiko murmured might have been "Oh God, oh God." If so, why? Whatever the reason, he needed to help her. But what should he do?

The doctor examined Tokiko, after Shunsuke informed him of her condition. "Tell me what happened," he said, directing his question to Shunsuke. "Does she have pain? I can give her something to relieve it, but I can't do much more. The doctor at the hospital wouldn't want me to interfere."

"I've been injecting her with male hormone every three days," Shunsuke told the doctor.

"That's fine."

"I wonder if you wouldn't mind giving it to her today. She's supposed to have an injection today."

"Certainly. I don't mind, but I don't think it has metastasized to the lung. If it had, she'd be having a lot more pain."

Shunsuke watched the doctor's hands intently, as though clinging to them.

⌒

Walking the doctor down the slope, Shunsuke framed in his mind the question he wanted to ask the doctor: Is it best not to mention religion to a patient in my wife's situation? What actually came out of his mouth, however, was different: "Domestic help is hard to come by these days. Do you have the same problem with your nurses?"

"I've brought a nurse from my hometown, and my wife helps out, too. I don't actually like big cities. We came to Tokyo for our children's education."

The conversation then turned to the man who went through the neighborhood selling fresh fish. The doctor said he would tell the fishmonger to stop at Shunsuke's house.

Three

*T*ōkiko was readmitted to the hospital in early July, several months after her first visit to Dr. K. This time she insisted on taking a few items with her, and she dispatched Shunsuke to buy them.

"The nurses are complaining that your wife is spoiled," Dr. K remarked to Shunsuke one day. "They say she has her own refrigerator and electric fan. So I told them I gave her permission. Nurses are like petty bureaucrats these days. I have to remind them that their job is to look after sick people."

"I'm grateful," Shunsuke said, lowering his head.

"Now, I've already told your wife this, but you mustn't stay more than a few hours each day," the doctor continued. "Actually, an hour is best, but you should come every day."

~

The surgery was performed, and a course of chemotherapy followed. As expected, Tokiko lost her appetite, and she had to be fed intravenously. Seeing food on a tray was enough to make her groan.

Despite what the doctor recommended, Shunsuke went to the hospital before lunch and stayed until evening, sometimes until nine o'clock, leaving only to buy whatever food Tokiko fancied. But whatever he returned with would be met with only a disinterested look out of the corner of her eye.

↩

On the train one day, not long after Tokiko's surgery, Shunsuke overheard two housewives talking about making wine and pickles from the season's harvest of plums. Shunsuke had a vague recollection that the family's plum tree was laden with fruit. And for equally vague reasons, he was motivated when he got home to ask Masako to make pickles from the plums. Masako displayed little knowledge of or interest in the task.

Shunsuke and Ryoichi, wearing boots on the muddy, sloped ground, picked the fruit on the tree's tangled branches. A good part of the crop had already fallen to the ground. Using a recipe he found, Shunsuke proceeded to make the pickles himself, spending several days at it. When done, he placed the jar of pickles to cure in a corner of the tool shed.

"Why in the world does the old man want to make pickles this year?" Ryoichi asked Masako.

"Does the Master like plum pickles, or is this a hobby of his?"

"He's never made them before. Mom will be upset when she hears about this."

"Why would she? I don't see why."

"He's just trying to make more work for you and me."

"But why would that upset Madam?"

"Because he's useless," Ryoichi said.

With the windows of the house sealed tight, noises from the street were effectively shut out. Sounds inside the house, however, traveled freely through the hallway, the stairway, and the wall ducts. The television, the radio, and all conversations could be clearly heard. Shunsuke had heard this conversation clearly.

↩

It did not please Shunsuke to see Masako cheerful or Ryoichi acting as if he had been set free. Admittedly, the fact that Tokiko wasn't in the house gave Shunsuke a sense of relief, but he did not want to see that relief in his son. Ryoichi needs to feel unhappy, Shunsuke thought; that is the only way this household will stay together.

"Ryoichi," he called downstairs, "you said you were going to the hospital today."

"Yeah, Dad," Ryoichi said, looking up at his father at the top of the stairs.

"What do you have in your hand?"

"This?" Ryoichi held up his mother's diamond ring. "Mom wanted me to bring it to her."

"Is she going to wear it?"

"I guess so. I don't know. How should I know?" Ryoichi answered. Then he added, "Dad, you should know that Masako is a little unhappy. She might leave unless you treat her right. Since Mom isn't around, she asks me about what needs to be done."

Shunsuke thought he must buy her something, give a present.

↶

When Ryoichi stepped out of the hospital elevator, he saw his mother walking unsteadily toward him, as if moving through water. She was wearing her nightgown, but the slippers she had on were for outside use. Her steps were slow and deliberate.

Tokiko pretended she didn't see her son, stopping by the door of a large room and speaking, smiling, to the woman inside. The woman was in her seventies.

"Mom," said Ryoichi.

Tokiko continued talking without acknowledging him.

"Are you going to the bathroom, Mom?"

No response.

Ryoichi waited for his mother in her room. When Tokiko returned, the first words she said were: "Go . . . and ask that . . . old woman . . . to come. I'm going . . . to treat her . . . to watermelon." She spoke slowly, stopping after every few words, then got back into bed.

When the elderly woman arrived, Tokiko smiled, as she held her arms around her chest to ease her breathing.

"This is . . . for . . . you . . ."

"Thank you. Is this your son?" The elderly woman turned to Ryoichi. "Your mother has been so kind to me."

"Go ahead . . . eat," Tokiko said. "You can . . . talk . . . while . . . you . . . eat . . . Don't . . . worry about . . . the nurses."

"Thank you very much. You are so kind."

The elderly woman had had a part of her stomach removed, and when she'd been in a two-bed room, she would occasionally make her way past Tokiko's room, her head up, one hand on her chest, and, for some reason, holding a bucket in the other.

"Do you know," the elderly woman said after a few bites of watermelon, "I'm hungry all the time. They say my recovery is unusually fast. By comparison, my roommate has hardly improved. She doesn't want to use the bedpan, she insists on getting up and going to the bathroom. No wonder she hasn't gotten well. I bet she has cancer and doesn't know it. When I have visitors, she stares at me, and when I use the bedpan, she turns her face away. That's why the gods have given up on her, and she won't get well. I have a stomach ulcer."

The elderly woman turned to look at Ryoichi again. She said again to Tokiko what a nice son he was.

"I shouldn't . . . be here," Tokiko said. "Nothing . . . is wrong . . . with me . . . They . . . misdiagnosed me . . . you see . . . and they operated. On top of it . . . they gave me . . . radiation. My breasts . . . were sore . . . and then . . ."

"Your complexion is good," said the elderly woman, who, having finished the watermelon, smiled at Tokiko.

"Yes . . . I've always . . . been strong. I'll be . . . all right . . . even if . . . I don't eat . . . for a while. The head nurse . . . told me . . . it depends . . . how well you ate . . . when you were . . . healthy . . . that's what . . . she said."

The elderly woman nodded.

"When . . . I go home . . . you must . . . come to see . . . me . . . My house . . . is . . . cool in the . . . summer. Ryoichi . . . give her . . . our address . . ."

A nurse walked into the room, and the elderly woman rose to leave.

"You . . . don't have . . . to go."

"You'll tire yourself, Mrs. Miwa," the nurse said to Tokiko.

After the elderly woman had gone, Tokiko spoke vacantly to Ryoichi. "That old woman . . ." she said, "she . . . doesn't know . . . she has stomach cancer. She'll . . . be back here . . . I'm sure." She then looked at her son. "Why . . . are you . . . so . . . irritated? Don't come if you . . . don't want to . . . come . . . Don't come."

When she began to complain of the pain, Ryoichi handed her the diamond ring and hurried out of the room. Maybe I am not a good son, he said to himself, but I can't stand this.

࿐

"I don't like the way her legs are so dry," Dr. K was saying to Shunsuke in his office, "but the medication seems to be working, and the metastasis is being checked. I'm going to write up her case in a medical journal. The most important thing now is for her to eat. I tell her so, but her response is, 'Of course I want to eat, but you have to make me want to eat. How can I eat when you make me unable to eat?' She says I'm unreasonable. It's a difficult situation."

The conversation was interrupted by a pharmacist.

"By the way, Mr. Miwa," Dr. K said, once the pharmacist had gone, "there's been a complaint from the nurses."

"Complaint?" Shunsuke asked, suppressing his anger. "What about? Is it because I go to the nurse station and ask for things for my wife?"

"No, it's not about you. It's about Mrs. Miwa. Please don't get upset. The nurses don't think your wife should be giving other patients soft drinks and expensive fruit from her private refrigerator."

"Oh, that," Shunsuke said, swallowing.

"And another thing. This is rather awkward, but this ring, please take it back home."

"How did you get it? Did someone steal it?"

Dr. K shook his head. "No, your wife gave it to the head nurse."

Shunsuke accepted the ring silently.

Dr. K laughed a little, patting Shunsuke on the back. "It must be hard to find time to do your writing," he said.

～

The two men walked down the hall to room 365, where the name plate read: Miwa Tokiko.

As he examined Tokiko, Dr. K said, smiling, "You look like you've got something to tell me, Mrs. Miwa . . . But Mrs. Miwa, it's nice to have your husband visit you every day; that way he won't have time to flirt with other women . . . You're healing very nicely."

"I must . . . I must," Tokiko said, with a touch of reproach.

"You must get well soon and be ready to, how should I put it, to fool around?" Dr. K said, then roared with laughter. "The patient in Room 367 is trying very hard to get better; she's got a hole drilled in her skull, you know."

"I heard . . . she's on her . . . second marriage," Tokiko said with a flirtatious look, fighting for her breath. "How . . . long . . . does she . . . have?"

"She'll be all right for a time, maybe for a long time. But you mustn't ask such questions. You should try not to think that way. I don't think that way myself," Dr. K said under his breath. "And Mrs. Miwa, please do not peek into her room." The doctor said this somewhat sternly, but when he left the room, he was whistling lightly.

↝

Mrs. Otani was the patient in Room 367. Tokiko often stopped by her room along the way to the bathroom. At times she invited Mrs. Otani's caregiver to come by for fruit and food she herself couldn't eat.

One day, when the caregiver was in the corridor, Tokiko asked Shunsuke to invite her in.

The caregiver's eyes were red. "Mrs. Otani's sleeping now," she said. "She was awake all night last night. It won't be long . . ." She bowed and left quietly.

"It won't be . . . long," Tokiko repeated softly. "There were . . . a lot of . . . people there . . . the other day . . . singing . . . hymns."

"Yes, I saw them too."

↝

Shunsuke never knew how to act when he ran into Mrs. Otani's husband in the corridor. Sometimes he simply said hello; other times he pretended to be distracted by something.

↝

"I want . . . to go home . . . and soak in . . . a bath. At home . . . I can eat. If I stay . . . here . . . I'll get . . . worse. I'm going to . . . go home . . . at the end . . . of the month. I'm . . . fine . . . now. What I . . . need is . . . good food . . . and I want you . . . to make . . . love to me . . ."

"I'll ask the doctor, and we'll do what's best," Shunsuke replied, wondering how to persuade her not to leave the hospital.

"I can . . . tell . . . when you're . . . coming . . . by the . . . sound of . . . your . . . footsteps."

"You can?"

"Yes . . . you . . . drag one . . . foot." Tokiko grinned.

"Like this?" Shunsuke demonstrated with one leg straight and the other held wide.

"Don't . . . be silly."

Tokiko stuck out her leg to Shunsuke; she wanted him to massage it. "I . . . have to . . . go home . . . soon. I can't . . . trust Masako. She'll . . . get . . . our . . . new house . . . dirty."

⟷

As he passed by Room 367 one day, Shunsuke noticed a chain of tiny origami cranes hanging from the ceiling. Attached to the end of the chain was a slip of paper with calligraphy. Unable to read it at first glance, Shunsuke walked by the room three times until he managed to figure out what it said. It said: "For my wife whom I love most on this earth and in this universe."

When did he write that? Shunsuke wondered. Perhaps shortly after Mrs. Otani was admitted? He'd seen Mr. Otani with his wife at the clinic two and half months ago, in early May. She was hospitalized shortly afterward.

Shunsuke continued to Tokiko's room. Michiyo, their former maid, was coming out of the room.

"Hello," he whispered. It was a habit he had adopted since coming to the hospital; his voice was so low it was almost inaudible. He felt he could discourage others from talking loudly by doing so.

"I didn't know. Has she been sick for a while?'"

Shunsuke looked straight into Michiyo's eyes.

"I brought some custard for her, but I'm not sure if she'll like it."

Shunsuke nodded.

"How long has she been ill?"

"Since the time you moved out," Shunsuke replied tersely.

"This time I am really disgusted with that boy," Michiyo said, as if in a different conversation.

"What boy?"

"George, of course. No matter what I said, he wouldn't come to see Mrs. Miwa. He acts like a big shot these days, living in high style. He's got no excuse. Mrs. Miwa treated him so well . . . She's lost quite a lot of weight.'"

"Not that much," Shunsuke answered with a sour expression, which he maintained until Michiyo turned and left.

⌒

"Let's see . . . what she . . . brought," Tokiko said, opening the gift from Michiyo. Shunsuke took the lid off the Pyrex container and brought a spoonful of the custard to her mouth.

Tokiko moved her head away. "It looks . . . so heavy."

"Shall I throw it away?"

There was no reply.

"I'll put it in the refrigerator."

"When I . . . get home, I'll invite . . . everyone . . . to our . . . New Year's . . . dinner . . . Let them . . . taste my . . . superior cooking."

⌒

While Shunsuke was in a department store picking things up for Tokiko, he found himself facing a mannequin wearing a negligee, which flowed like a wedding gown. The thought of Tokiko wearing something like that excited him. He forgot that she was in a hospital, that she was a sick, aging wife; that she looked like a withered branch. For a moment he was under the illusion that she was fresh and healthy and twenty years younger.

"It's for my wife. Do you have any suggestions?"

"This would be nice for your wife," said the salesclerk, who might have been twenty-five or twenty-six.

"How about this pink one? Do you think it's too bright? Not-so-young ladies wear these colors nowadays, don't they? After all, it's for sleeping."

"I agree. Age isn't a consideration when it comes to lingerie. Pink is fine. Westerners wear bright colors nicely. I'm sure your wife would too. Besides, pretty colors are best for the bedroom."

Shunsuke carried on his conversation with the salesclerk as if he had a young, healthy wife at home.

ç

Tokiko had just slipped into the pink negligee when a young nurse came in to take her temperature. "Mrs. Miwa," she said, "you look so young today."

Tokiko ignored her and fanned herself. "Masako . . . she's no good," she said, speaking to Shunsuke in a low voice. "Only interested . . . in dolling . . . herself . . . up. When I . . . sent her . . . on an errand . . . it took her . . . three hours. She's like . . . a rabbit . . . running around . . . aimlessly. I'm not . . . sure . . . what she's . . . up to. I told her . . . so, and . . . then she . . . cried . . . like a child."

"Shall I take your clothes home for her to wash?" asked Shunsuke.

"She came . . . here . . . with something . . . dangling . . . around her neck . . . and her expression . . . changed . . . when a doctor . . . came in. You tell her . . . and Ryoichi . . . I don't want . . . them . . . to come see me . . . anymore."

Masako must have been wearing the pendant he'd given her, Shunsuke thought. Had she really come to the hospital with it on?

ç

Shunsuke recognized a certain sense of freedom in himself; it was subtle but he felt it acutely. It came to him when he was shopping for things he needed, when he was walking toward the store and talking to the salesclerk there; it came to him when he was startled by the faces of passersby, when he gazed at the darkened leaves and shrubs, when faint breezes touched his cheek, and when he unexpectedly found himself on a quiet lane with high-rises on both sides. On those occasions, he had the distinct feeling that he was alive.

"My wife is ill, critically ill, and I am her husband," he had wanted to cry out when he was out on the street earlier, but now, it was more of an urge to seek help. "We're all together, and our lives are uncertain and filled with pain. I am a man shopping, but please don't just take me for a man shopping. I want to relate to you all as a human being, and that's why I'm addressing you like this. We don't know each other, and yet we must communicate, because otherwise, what will become of us?"

Why do I feel like shouting to my fellow shoppers like this, and why does it only happen when I'm shopping? he wondered. Shunsuke had no idea.

౿

When he entered Tokiko's room one afternoon, Shunsuke was greeted by an elderly woman eating food from Tokiko's tray. Tokiko must have offered it to her. He watched her stuffing her mouth, thinking that she must be the woman Ryoichi had mentioned.

"You must be Mr. Miwa," the old woman said, bowing deeply.

"When will you be going home?" he asked her.

"My daughter-in-law will be here soon to take me home. I've just eaten my lunch, and I'm already hungry."

"You have . . . my address . . . don't you? And . . . my . . . telephone number . . . Be sure . . . to call . . . and come to . . . see me. We'll make . . . a nice . . . dinner," Tokiko said from her bed.

"You are so kind, like a goddess. You're the only person here who treated me like her own relative," she said, bowing deeply again. She then removed a piece of paper from the pocket of her shabby bathrobe.

"This is my telephone number, Madam."

There was a voice from the corridor.

"My daughter-in-law is here," the elderly woman said, standing up and walking slowly out the door.

ↄ

"If . . . I go home, I can . . . eat. An old . . . woman like her . . . can, so . . ." Tokiko moaned.

A young ward doctor walked in.

"You look . . . cheerful . . . today, Doctor," said Tokiko to him, smiling eagerly.

"I see you've had your guest again," the doctor said, grinning. "And you're in a good mood, too. Did anything good happen?"

"Dr. K said . . . I can go . . . home soon. He's not . . . mean . . . like you."

"I see." The young doctor smiled, looking at Shunsuke.

"I can't . . . eat because . . . the hospital food is terrible. And I . . . must eat . . . you see."

"You want to go home that badly?" The young doctor was not smiling anymore. "It's all right with me. You can do what Dr. K said."

Shunsuke listened to the exchange between the two without a word.

"I should . . . be much . . . better by . . . now. So . . ."

"You're right. If you can complain like this, it proves you are fine. You're a funny lady, Mrs. Miwa," said the doctor.

When he left, Tokiko said, "He's no good . . . so vague." She gave Shunsuke a sharp look. "Have you . . . arranged . . . the gift of beer . . . to be delivered . . . to his office?"

"It should be there by now," he said, walking away from her bed. "I'll stop by and check on my way out."

                                                    *

One hot afternoon, when the curtain was fluttering at the window, Shimizu, a young family friend for whom the Miwas had once acted as a matchmaker, came to see Tokiko. It was he who had recommended Dr. K to them.

"Don't forget . . . to treat your wife . . . well . . . Mr. Shimizu."

"I know," answered Shimizu seriously.

"It's . . . no good . . . to do it . . . when it's too late . . . like my husband . . . here. It's when . . . the children . . . are young . . . we women need . . . husbands . . . at home."

Shunsuke, with a smile on his face, kept examining the blood transfusion equipment.

                                                    *

Tokiko, who had set her mind on going home at the end of two months, insisted on having her way, believing that she would get well if she went home and ate. She ignored the doctor's opinion, and when the day arrived, she had her belongings organized and her face made up. She was ready to go.

With Tokiko's suitcases, Shunsuke was waiting at the entrance of the hospital for their hired car when he saw Mr. Otani emerging from a taxi. Mr. Otani approached him and asked if Tokiko was going home. It was the first time Shunsuke and he had spoken.

"She'll probably have to come back again, but since she insists . . . I'm not sure what'll happen," Shunsuke said.

Mr. Otani said nothing and hurried into the building. He went up the stairway, and as Shunsuke watched, Mr. Otani lost his footing and fell, grabbing the railing. From a distance it appeared as if he had fallen deliberately. Shunsuke was about to run to him, but Mr. Otani picked himself up and proceeded up the stairs, his body bent over a little. The hired car arrived just then, and Shunsuke went back to Tokiko's room.

He was walking with Tokiko, almost carrying her, when he saw Miss Nishimura, Dr. K's nurse, come running toward them.

"Wait there!" she cried. "I'll get a wheelchair. She shouldn't walk."

She settled Tokiko into the wheelchair and pushed her to the hospital entrance. "Mr. Miwa," she said, "please lend me a hand." Then, she put Tokiko into the car.

"Please . . . come to . . . see me. My house is . . . a bit . . . unusual as . . . I . . . told you. Promise me . . . you'll . . . come . . . I'll be . . . well . . . by then."

"I understand she was given her medicine, so she might become nauseated," the nurse said to Shunsuke. She bowed deeply as the car drove off.

"Honey . . . when we get . . . back . . . I want . . ." Tokiko said, trailing off as the car headed homeward. In the last several months, her facial hair had thickened and her voice had taken on a metallic tone, resembling that of an adolescent boy's. Without her trying, it was low, and for unaccustomed ears it was hard to make out what she was saying. Not only did Shunsuke hear her, however, he knew exactly what she meant by "I want . . ."

He squeezed her hand, and she squeezed back. It was a very weak squeeze, and her hand, rather large for a woman, held his awkwardly. After a while, she let go in order to reach into her purse for a handkerchief. Seeing the way her hand shook, Shunsuke knew a fit of coughing was coming.

⌡

Masako greeted them as they got out of the car.

"Thank you," Tokiko said, smiling. She walked toward the house on her own.

"How pretty . . . the goldfish. And . . . the water lilies . . . so beautiful," she said. She beamed as she stepped into the house.

After she had settled into bed, she said to Shunsuke, who stood by her, "You've lost . . . some weight. You look . . . better now." Her eyes were bright.

With considerable difficulty, and as if in defiance, Tokiko soaked in the bath she'd been longing for. Shunsuke washed her with Noriko's help. Then, Tokiko started coughing, and was barely able to breathe. "Please, honey . . . I don't care if it . . . kills me," she said between coughing and labored breathing.

Although he could scarcely bear to see her like that, Shunsuke and Tokiko went to bed, and he let himself enter her, become one with her, piercingly and with a sadness that was reflected in his expression. Did Mr. Otani, who had written the words "For my wife whom I love most on this earth and in this universe," go through this too? Had he thought the same thoughts?

A few minutes later, Shunsuke rang the neighborhood doctor who had attended Tokiko earlier.

Six weeks after her return home, an angry Tokiko was carried into the taxi, accompanied by Shunsuke and the neighborhood doctor, who kept his fingers on her pulse. The taxi headed toward the hospital in Shunjuku. After twenty minutes in the car, Tokiko pointed to the adjacent car and laughed, "Look over there, it's Noriko." Her daughter and son were riding in a separate taxi, which was about to overtake theirs.

As soon as she was settled in the hospital bed, Tokiko asked for her purse. She applied some makeup, and then, needing to move her bowels, insisted she get out of bed.

"You shouldn't get up," the nurse said.

"Never . . . mind, I'm . . . getting . . . up."

"Please. Use the bedpan and save your strength."

"Do as I . . . tell you. Hold me . . . here."

The nurse was aghast.

With help from the nurse, Shunsuke managed to get Tokiko to the toilet, but the next time when she wanted to get up, it wasn't possible. An oxygen tube was inserted into her nose.

Shunsuke stayed with Tokiko for four days and nights until the caregiver he'd hired arrived.

"You have a full time attendant now, and so I can't stay here at night," he told Tokiko.

"You were . . . here only . . . one day," she mumbled.

"I was here for four days," he told Tokiko.

"You are . . . lying."

"Really, I have been here for four days."

"Sometimes . . . you tell . . . transparent lies . . . I can see right . . . through you."

Shunsuke burst into laughter, shaking. He realized then that Tokiko had been given morphine. He still couldn't stop laughing, and the laughter made him look like he had really lied.

Tokiko didn't ask about Mrs. Otani. If she doesn't ask today, she won't ask at all, Shunsuke thought. She probably knew: Mrs. Otani had died the month before.

~

A few days later, Shunsuke went to a department store to buy diapers for Tokiko. When he brought back medium-sized diapers, the caregiver, a woman near Tokiko's age, said, "Large would be better. Even though Mrs. Miwa is thin, she has a large frame. Large is easier to use anyway."

"Would you like me to go get some large ones?"

"I think you should get two packs. Also, there's no more antiseptic solution, and I need some flannel to make into a waistcloth."

"Anything else?"

Tokiko lay in bed with her eyes open, but she was not awake.

⌁

There was something else Shunsuke wanted to buy. Tokiko no longer wore the pink negligee, which he had taken home to be washed, and she had asked him for a robe. She needed it to put over her shoulders when sitting up in bed or, in case she was able to get up, when going to the bathroom.

When Shunsuke was out shopping once, he had seen in a store window a robe with a checkered pattern that he thought would look good on Tokiko. But when he inquired about it, he was told that the style was sold out. Shunsuke was determined to find her a checker-patterned robe. Now that he had to go buy more diapers, he thought he would try again.

At the department store, Shunsuke was told that the large-sized diapers were also sold out but that there would be a delivery in three hours.

"Are they for a man or a woman," asked the salesclerk.

"A woman, for my wife," Shunsuke said, his voice rising.

"What's her frame like?"

"What do you mean? She's very sick and needs to wear diapers. In any case, I want large-sized diapers."

"Large?" the salesclerk asked with a sneer, responding to Shunsuke's aggressive tone.

"Why don't you keep the large size in stock? They're the most in demand."

"We keep them in our Kanda warehouse."

"That's ridiculous." Shunsuke was furious.

"We keep them in Kanda, I said."

"I'll be back in three hours. Please be sure they're here."

As he walked away from the counter, Shunsuke found himself stopping and staring each time he passed a woman of Tokiko's age. He stared until the woman would disappear into a crowd.

Ah, she's like a soft cake . . . There's flesh over her bones, he thought to himself. And all these women have their own husbands and children.

On the floor where fabrics were sold, Shunsuke discovered several mannequins dressed in kimonos. Indeed, in this world there are creatures called women who wear these beautiful garments, he said to himself. Was it really true that one of them had been with him, had talked to him, had been jealous of him, and he of her? Was it true that she had shared a bed with him?

When Shunsuke approached the lingerie department, he was surprised to find a mannequin outfitted in a robe with a checkered pattern. The same woman who had sold him the pink negligee was at the counter.

"That negligee looked very nice on my wife," Shunsuke said to her. The woman's faint, sweet fragrance filled his nostrils; his spirits rose a little. "You know, some salesclerks can be rather unpleasant."

"In which department was this, sir?"

"Well . . . it doesn't matter. Do you have a robe like that one over there?" he asked, narrowly escaping having to explain about the diapers.

"Let me see . . . Yes, how about this one?"

"That's a little . . ." said Shunsuke, shaking his head. There was too much red and not enough green.

"It's for your wife, isn't it?"

"Yes, it is. She's in the hospital."

"Oh, you must be worried. Shall I show you this one then?" Assisted by her colleague, the salesclerk started to undress the mannequin. "Do you mind turning around for a second?" she asked Shunsuke.

Shunsuke did not immediately understand what the saleclerk meant, but then it occurred to him. "Oh, yes, of course," he said. This was just like the nurses at the hospital changing Tokiko's night-clothes.

As the clerks removed the robe from the mannequin, the manne-quin's arm hit the counter. The sound caused Shunsuke to turn back, and he watched the clerks going about their task with a fascination mixed with relief. In fact, it was a feeling of well-being similar to what he experienced when he observed women absorbed in house-hold chores, like cooking dishes late into the night for the new year's celebration, or restuffing the bedding.

"She's bedridden now, so she'll just put it over her shoulders. But someday she may be able to . . ."

"I'm sure she will. This one might be good for young people, but it all depends on how one feels. I think this will be nice for your wife."

"I only hope she lives, and then . . . There're so many things I want to talk over with her."

This woman doesn't ask what illness Tokiko is suffering from, said Shunsuke to himself. His voice lowered as he chatted on, telling her things she didn't need to know. "I couldn't find this robe at other stores. I live with my son and daughter and a maid. My son doesn't want to visit his mother at the hospital. He quarrels about it with his sister. She's very good to her mother—talking to her, giving her massages, and always smiling. But my son, he only makes faces."

❧

When Shunsuke returned the hospital, Tokiko asked that the fluid be drained from her chest. Shunsuke replied that it had just been done. Tokiko then wanted him to help her sit up in bed. Once she was sitting up, she put her face down on the quilt. In this posi-tion, she mumbled something. Shunsuke brought his ear close to her face to hear what she was saying.

"I think . . . I . . . was . . . wrong," she was saying. "Why . . . I thought . . . I could . . . stay home . . ."

Shunsuke put away the new robe without showing it to her.

"Mrs. Otani died," he said. The words just came out.

"No . . . she didn't," Tokiko mumbled, her face still down.

She asked Shunsuke to help lift her upper body. "Be gentle . . ." she complained. "Why . . . are you . . . looking at me . . . like that . . . ?"

Is it possible that Tokiko, who was so good at finding out everything, didn't know about Mrs. Otani's death? Had she not heard about it from the nurses or from her caregiver?

"You're going to be fine," he said, walking over to the window. "There are other treatments to try. Dr. K is waiting for the best time."

Tokiko's room overlooked a tennis court, and Shunsuke could see Dr. K and Miss Nishimura, his nurse, in the middle of a match, talking and laughing. Shunsuke watched them play. Dr. K hit a ball over the fence and into the alley; it kept rolling, ending up near where a cinema was located. The doctor climbed the fence and looked for the ball; he couldn't see it.

"Where did it go?" he was asking Nishimura.

"Over there!" Shunsuke couldn't keep himself from calling out, although they couldn't hear him. When Shunsuke turned around, he saw Tokiko with her eyes wide open and very still. When he turned back to the tennis court, Dr. K was practicing his swing while waiting for the nurse to retrieve the ball.

❧

Around nine that night, two doctors came into Tokiko's room, looking cheerful. They were dressed in suits, not their usual white coats, and they seemed to have been drinking.

"Is she sleeping?" Dr. K asked.

Shunsuke nodded and stood up. The two doctors exchanged a few words in German, while studying the patient's face.

"Why don't you go home, Mr. Miwa," Dr. K said, moving closer to the bed. "We've given her morphine. She wouldn't be able to tolerate the medication otherwise. By the way, I spoke to a doctor in Germany this afternoon. We've been sharing data, and he was pleased to hear how our research has been going."

"I see," Shunsuke said. He smiled.

"He mentioned a new medicine, which is supposed to be very effective. I asked him to send us some."

"How long will it take to get here?"

"I'm not sure, but it shouldn't be long."

"Where was it, the meeting you've been at?" Shunsuke asked, wishing the doctor would use the new drugs on Tokiko right away.

"At the Hotel Okura. It was a big medical convention."

"You were playing tennis today. I saw you from the window here."

"Oh, did you see us?" Dr. K looked uncomfortable. "We've had some complaints about playing during working hours, but since we have no other time . . . Do you play tennis?"

"No, I don't."

"Well, it's a good game. But Mr. Miwa, you should go home now."

Shunsuke was about to leave when he remembered something. "Wait a minute, Doctor," Shunsuke said. "I don't want to be presumptuous, but please accept this." He handed Dr. K an envelope.

"What is it?" Dr. K asking, opening the envelope. It was a bank draft. "You know, this really isn't necessary."

"I appreciate all you're doing, so . . ."

"I'm trying my best, Mr. Miwa," the doctor replied with a smile.

ↄ

Stepping into Tokiko's room, Shunsuke saw two nuns whispering into her ears; they looked like crows picking at grain.

"What are you doing here? Get out! Please leave!" Shunsuke shouted.

"Yes . . . yes, we're about to leave," one nun said, although they did not go immediately. Then, backing out of the room, they looked Shunsuke in the face for the first time. One of them, under her black hood, had the yellowish face of an old woman with glasses; the other was a young woman with rosy cheeks.

Unable to calm himself down, Shunsuke ran down the corridor after them. "Wait a minute, wait a minute!" he shouted, causing the nurses pushing food carts to turn around. "I know you've been in that room before. How can you do that without being asked? I don't think the hospital allows that." Shunsuke spoke loud enough so that the nurses would hear.

"We apologize. Please don't raise your voice," the older nun said. She extended her hand to him, nodding, as if trying to soothe a child.

"'This is inexcusable!" Shunsuke said angrily.

"Please. Don't be so upset . . . for your own sake."

"Don't worry about me!" Shunsuke was furious. The nun's concern made him even more angry.

"You are very tired," said the younger nun gently, which took him by surprise. "You are under terrible stress. Your wife has such serenity, but you . . . you look so tense, so fierce. Is there anything we can do for you?"

"Do you mean I look like I'm dying?" Shunsuke regretted saying those words the second he uttered them. The older nun pulled at the sleeve of the younger nun, wanting to leave. But the younger nun, under her hood and with her eyes closed, simply nodded. "Yes, you do," she said. She seemed like she was waiting be kissed.

Still seething, Shunsuke felt drained. He tried to calm himself down. He put his ear to Tokiko's mouth, just as he had seen the nuns do.

"I'm . . . all right . . . even if . . . they are . . . here," Tokiko whispered gently, and then fell into sleep.

"Do I really look so fierce, Tokiko?" he whispered to his wife, squeezing her hand, now so thin, when it had always been larger than his. There was no response. She had been given morphine.

⌁

Two weeks later, Shunsuke went to see Dr. K.

"Well?" Dr. K turned from his desk and faced Shunsuke as if he was going to examine him.

"Tokiko's doctor at the hospital told me that it would be a week or ten days." He sounded like he was choking. "Is that how long she has?"

"Did he say that?" Dr. K looked into Shunsuke's eyes, trying to read his mind. "He said that? I can't be so sure. It may be a month, maybe two. I will do my best to keep her alive for that length of time. But it is true that your wife is now at the stage where you should start preparing yourself."

"Is it possible to try the new drug you once mentioned, the one you experimented with on mice?"

"Oh that." Dr. K scratched his head. "To tell the truth, we've run out of the drug. We've had some resignations in lab personnel, and now we don't have the staff to do the job. I've read about a drug that extended a patient's life up to seven months, but I'm afraid we have no money to test it."

Shunsuke did not have the heart to ask about the drug the German doctor was supposed to be sending.

"Then there's nothing you can do?" Shunsuke muttered, feeling angry. When Tokiko first saw Dr. K, it was clear that she would not live another nine months. Why didn't I realize that? he berated himself.

"I'm afraid there's nothing more I can do. By the way," Dr. K went on, "the other day, I saw a television show called *Dr. Kildare*."

"I saw it too."

"Did you? In that show, the patient is hooked up to a machine so that the heart keeps going even after it should have stopped. The show is fictional, but I thought it raised an important question. In my opinion, it is a physician's duty to prolong his patient's life."

Shunsuke nodded, but he wasn't asking the doctor to consider such an approach. He wasn't in fact asking anything; he was having a hard time dealing with the shock of knowing that Tokiko would soon be dead. It occurred to him that he was totally unprepared for it.

"It must be very hard," said the doctor. He, too, seemed angry.

Shunsuke didn't answer.

"It's not my area of expertise, but a wife and husband are not blood relations after all," the doctor continued.

"That's true."

"The question is how your children will cope. They are related to their mother by blood."

Shunsuke remained silent. After a pause, he asked, "Do the nuns visit patients on instructions from the doctors?"

"No, but without us telling them, it's clear which patients are terminal. A 'No Visitors' sign on the door tells them. We simply don't stop them. Some patients welcome that kind of approach."

"But isn't treatment more effective if those people aren't around?"

"Treatment?" the doctor replied with a smile on his face. "Mr. Miwa, we are in no stage of treatment now. We are giving morphine to your wife so she does not feel pain. Is there anything else you want to ask?"

"No."

"It's you who needs care now, Mr. Miwa."

Shunsuke stood up and stumbled out of the doctor's office.

و

Despite their difficulties, Tokiko had always been the person Shunsuke would turn to talk to. Now that he no longer could, he felt the need more urgently. For the first time in his many years of marriage, he longed to communicate with her.

Why did he not believe she was dying? Was it because she was still alive? She was thin as a mummy, and yet he had not really seen it, not understood it, because she was there in front of him, still alive. It had been clear for the last six months, for the last year, that Tokiko was going to die soon, but he had never accepted that. How did this appear to other people? It didn't matter, but had both he and Tokiko been under the same illusion?

He thought of his new house made of concrete and steel. He felt it subject to the disdain of those around him. He felt regret and grief. He felt affection for the old house he had once hated.

As he approached the narrow, busy lane where he walked every day, Shunsuke saw a woman, who seemed charming and familiar, walking toward him. He stopped in his path and stared at her, trying to remember who she was. Then he bowed and proceeded a few steps toward the specialty food store where he had been shopping regularly, where he had bought baby food the day before.

"Who is she?" he asked himself.

Suddenly it came to him. She was the salesclerk who had sold him the checker-patterned robe. He turned around and their eyes met; apparently she had stopped and turned around too.

"My wife is no longer . . ." Words were coming out of his mouth to tell her.

⌐

At the crowded subway station, Shunsuke searched for a telephone. Ten phones were lined up by the information booth, and people stood in various postures as they made their calls. No one showed any sign of relinquishing their phone. Finally, he saw a person hanging up, but as he walked toward that phone, a woman got there before him, leaving him with the moist scent of her perfume. He waited again, gazing into the air. He wasn't sure if he really wanted to make the calls.

When a phone next became available, Shunsuke stepped toward it like a robot, but someone who looked like a salesman got to it first. The man's elbow met his chest. Shunsuke stopped in his tracks and looked vacantly around him, then at the open space through which he walked several times daily. As always, hundreds of people were hurrying back and forth, bustling about, all of them strangers.

Eventually, Shunsuke got to a phone. He called three friends who had come to see Tokiko at the hospital; the first two calls were answered by their wives, the last by a housekeeper. He wanted to thank them and tell them about Tokiko's condition, but no one could understand what he was saying. He tried to repeat himself more loudly, and when he did, he realized that the noise around him was not the problem; he had been mumbling. And speaking more loudly, he became confused, unsure of what he was saying.

⁓

For some time, Shunsuke had had the urge to shock his son into sensibility; it was the same kind of feeling he once had with Tokiko.

Ryoichi was watching television when Shunsuke got home. "Your mother doesn't have much longer to live," Shunsuke said to him.

"What do you mean?" Ryoichi said, turning to his father. "You said they were going to use a new drug."

"It's no use . . ."

"That's not what they told us," Ryoichi said. His voice was defiant.

"You have to prepare yourself."

"That's ridiculous. You've got to do something."

"What do you mean by that?"

"You've been sloppy, that's what I mean. It's the same thing with Masako."

"What about her?"

"Oh, never mind. I've been trying to keep her happy for all our sakes. But that's beside the point now." Ryoichi put his head in his hands. "How much longer?" he asked, looking up.

"A week. Maybe ten days."

"But didn't they say just the other day that she'd be stable for another month?"

"Where's Noriko?"

"Upstairs taking a nap."

"We'll have to tell her when she comes down."

"It's going to be hard on her," Ryoichi said.

"It will be, but you mustn't brood about it. Try to think of taking care of yourself from now on," said Shunsuke consolingly but with a tinge of nastiness. "At your age, you should be on your own. You ought to be ready to leave home, to be independent. Your mother's death will be an opportunity to grow up."

Ryoichi did not say a word. He looked up at his father, and then down at the floor.

"Don't dwell too heavily on her dying. If you do well living your own life, she'll live on within you."

"I know!" Ryoichi cried.

The strength of Ryoichi's voice astonished Shunsuke; it was his turn now to feel desperate.

"My mother isn't like other mothers. She never treated me like a grown-up."

"That's because you haven't shown her that you are."

"Maybe so, but other people's mothers are different."

"Really?" Shunsuke asked. "Well, since your mother won't be around soon, you'll have to grow up."

*

When he saw Noriko coming downstairs, Shunsuke felt his heart constricting.

"Dad, you look tired," Noriko said.

"Noriko," Shunsuke began, "you have to be brave. Your mother doesn't have much longer to live."

"Is that true?" Noriko turned her face away from her father.

Ryoichi looked at her searchingly.

"As you grow up, your mother will live on within you." Shunsuke repeated what he had said to his son. "Anyway, you should tell your teacher tomorrow, in case you have to be out of school."

Noriko nodded, saying nothing.

"Well, let's eat dinner. We need to cheer up!" Shunsuke said after a while.

Noriko ran crying to her room.

༄

After dinner Shunsuke went to the toolshed to check on his plum pickles. The pickles were ruined, rust having gotten into the jar. When Shunsuke showed the jar to the children, his voice cheerful but unsteady, Ryoichi responded disgustedly, "Plums."

The three family members returned to the house together, close on each other's heels.

༄

Masako stood in the middle of her room under the hanging lamp.

"I want to leave, Mr. Miwa," she said.

"Are you going back to your family?"

Masako did not answer.

"We need help rather badly just now. I don't want you to leave, not right now at least," he said. "Do you have another place to go to? Has someone offered you a job? Do you have a boyfriend?" Shunsuke spoke without lowering his voice.

Masako remained silent.

"Could you please stay with us for a little while? I'll see if we can accommodate your wishes, whatever they are."

When Masako nodded, Shunsuke felt like crying.

و

The next day when Shunsuke was at the hospital, Ryoichi called.

"Masako insists on leaving, and I don't want to have to be the one to persuade her to stay."

"Tell her to wait until I come home," Shunsuke said.

و

When Shunsuke got home, Ryoichi was sitting in a chair with his face buried in his hands. Masako was nowhere to be found.

Shunsuke phoned an agency and asked that someone, anyone, be sent over right away. Then he called Shimizu and asked if he could stay with the family for a while.

Shunsuke was in bed that night, lying with his eyes open in the darkness when Noriko came in.

"Dad—"

He sat up in his bed. "You can't sleep?"

Seeing his daughter standing there silent made him recall the times when Tokiko had come to his room the same way.

"Why don't you sleep here, then. I'll get the futon and some blankets for you. Or would you rather have my bed?"

"The futon is all right."

As Noriko was setting up her futon, Ryoichi came in with a letter in his hand. "Express mail for you, Dad."

Shunsuke saw his name, written in excellent calligraphy on the envelope. On the other side was the name and address of the sender, Ito Ayako. He did not recognize the name. As he read the letter, he felt the blood draining from his face.

"I heard you've been telling people that I chased after you like a crazed dog. That is very upsetting. I had no idea you would do such a thing. It was such a cruel betrayal. I thought you loved me in your own way. In your article 'The Way of a Modern Couple,' you wrote that a husband should try to meet his wife's needs, to be sensitive to her concerns. My husband said that you ought to be writing something less boring; I disagreed with him. But now, I think my husband was right. I think you are despicable."

One reason Shunsuke did not recognize the woman's name was her new address. She had moved away from Tokyo.

"C'mon, Dad, let's go to sleep," Noriko was saying.

"Yes, yes," Shunsuke said. But his mind was elsewhere, trying to recall whom he could have said these things to. It had been several years ago, and he couldn't remember anything. He crumpled up the letter, threw it into the wastebasket, and turned out the light.

"Noriko," he called out his daughter in the darkness. "Don't think too much about this. But if you feel like praying, pray for your mother's soul."

⌐

It was Sunday. Shunsuke listened to the tearful voice of Tokiko's caregiver on the phone, then quickly gathered the children together. Although the roads were not crowded, the taxi took fifty minutes to get to the hospital.

As Ryoichi dashed up the stairs ahead of him, Shunsuke asked, "Where is Noriko?"

"I think she went to the toilet," Ryoichi answered, panting at the top of the stairs. Noriko then appeared with a handkerchief in her hand.

"Where have you been?" Shunsuke asked.

Noriko, who was in her school uniform, replied with a smile, "In the ladies' room."

"It's not time for your period, is it?" he asked, realizing this was something her mother might have said.

"No, but I felt like I was going to pee in my pants," she said matter-of-factly.

"Dad," whispered Ryoichi, coming up to Shunsuke, "does Noriko know what death means?"

"I'm not sure. Do you?"

"Well, I don't know, but Noriko . . ."

"Let's hurry," Shunsuke called to his daughter, standing in the strangely vacant corridor, smoothing her hair. Then the three started to run.

When they got to Tokiko's room, they found her lying flat on her back in bed. "She passed away ten minutes after I called you," the caregiver said anxiously. "I am so sorry. It was so sudden I couldn't do anything."

"It's all right."

"She didn't suffer at the end."

"Is that true?"

"And she had a glass of milk this morning."

Ryoichi and Noriko cried out. Noriko burst into tears.

After some time, the nurse helped the children out of the room, and the caregiver prepared to take her leave.

"Thank you for all you've done for my wife," Shunsuke said. "I appreciate all your hard work. Please tell me how much I owe you."

Once the caregiver departed, the nurse asked Shunsuke to leave the room. "I have to do a few things before taking her down," she said. "Also, the doctor would like to see you."

When Shunsuke met the children standing by the door, he was momentarily startled. Here was his entire family—and yet there were only two Miwas present. "Three," he corrected himself a moment later: "Three Miwas." He hadn't counted himself.

As the three Miwas were running down the corridor earlier, the thought had occurred to Shunsuke that they must seem a bit comical;

they didn't look like they were running to a deathbed; more like kindergarten children in a race. He was reminded too of the time, ten years back, when Tokiko and the children had come to visit him in the hospital after his appendectomy. That was right after their first house was built. Tokiko had never seemed more confident.

~

"By all means, go ahead," he said in an overly eager manner when the doctor asked his permission for an autopsy. Autopsy anything you want, the whole body if you like, he wanted to add. Tokiko wouldn't have hesitated to give her consent. She was like that, and that was what was so good about her.

Shunsuke went down to the morgue, following the stretcher with Tokiko's body. When he returned to the room where the bed sat empty, he packed Tokiko's belongings into a suitcase. He deposited the children into a taxi in front of the hospital, and then returned to Tokiko's floor to discuss funeral arrangements. "Now, don't be stingy," he could hear Tokiko saying over his shoulder. Every time he had to make a decision, he would be asking silently: What would you do, Tokiko, if you were here?

~

There was about an hour before the wake at the hospital was to take place. Shunsuke stood in the corridor with tears in his eyes, turning around when he heard soft shuffling footsteps behind him. It was the two nuns walking nervously toward him.

"We've heard that your wife has passed away."

"I'm sorry about the other day," he mumbled.

"Please pray for her," the younger nun said.

"I have been praying. But I have no one to pray to. I will pray anyhow, and I will endure. All I can do is to think of the future."

"You are very close to God now, Mr. Miwa."

"Why?" he asked. "Because I've lost my wife? I've just completed a major task, and I did a messy job." He could feel his tears drying as he followed the nuns down the corridor. "I feel pity for my children. How are we going to go on? Even though I knew this would happen, it was still so unexpected."

Then, abruptly, he stopped talking. He bid the nuns good-bye and went out to the street. He went to the noodle shop where he had often eaten, where he had purchased noodles to take to Tokiko. The small space was filled with people holding their bowls up to their chins while keeping their eyes glued to the television screen. For them, this was a place to eat and relax.

The television commercial screeched: "Vita-mix for the fighting spirit! Increase your energy! With Vita-mix! With Vita-mix!"

Shunsuke felt his existence was less real than the images on the television set.

⁓

When he returned to the hospital, a security guard with alcohol on his breath handed him the key to the room where Tokiko's body was laid out. The guard's smile suggested he expected a tip. Shunsuke ignored him.

When he was about to leave the hospital after the wake, which ended at eight o'clock, Shunsuke spotted Dr. K at the entrance. His immediate reaction was to run the other away, but the doctor was walking toward him.

"How are you doing, Mr. Miwa?" the doctor asked. He was smiling and wearing a business suit. "I am very sorry," he said then.

"She tried very hard, though."

"Yes, she really did." The doctor then exchanged a few words with hospital staff passing by.

"Shall we go?" the doctor asked. They walked through a narrow lane bounded by high walls and came to where the cinema was located.

"It's always cool here on hot days," said Shunsuke, sounding as if his remark held some importance. While the doctor lit his cigarette, Shunsuke stood and waited.

"Kennedy's been assassinated, and that two-train collision in Tsurumi killed more than one hundred people," said the doctor as they passed a large loud pachinko parlor. "Things like that make me wonder why we physicians try so hard to prolong life."

"Life shouldn't be wasted."

"You're absolutely right, Mr. Miwa."

Despite his initial impulse to run, Shunsuke was now feeling that Dr. K was his sole source of consolation.

"Mr. Miwa," the doctor said, "the light is green. Shall we cross?"

"Yes. I'll pick up a taxi over there, and . . ."

Dr. K was already crossing the street ahead of him.

"I'll take this streetcar. Good night, Mr. Miwa." The doctor stepped onto the platform in the middle of the street and boarded the trolley. Shunsuke, who had expected the doctor to cross to the other side of the street with him, hurried on. He saw the doctor in the streetcar, looking up at an advertisement.

↩

When he got home, Shunsuke found about twenty people gathered in the living room; they rose as he came in. There had never been an occasion when so many people were in his house.

At noon the next day, Shunsuke and the children went to the hospital morgue for an informal service; among those present were friends who had visited Tokiko in the hospital. Each threw a chrysanthemum into the coffin, and at the last, Michiyo laid a bunch of chrysanthemums by Tokiko's face.

"Mr. Miwa, will you be having this beautiful face sketched?" Michiyo said.

"No, that can't be done."

"But she's going to be off on her journey with an immaculate heart, free of all pain. I'm sure you want to remember this expression."

"There's no need for that," said Shunsuke firmly. If her dead face has that quality, it must have been there before, too. His only worry now was how to help the children to cope with her absence.

Four

Mr. Miwa, you must be inconsolable in your sorrow," Michiyo
began, bowing to Shunsuke, who was sitting with his back
to the urn containing Tokiko's ashes. "You too, Ryoichi and Noriko.
Your home will be so lonely from now on."

"Thank you for all you've done for us," Shunsuke replied. Just
listening to Michiyo's words brought tears to his eyes.

"I wasn't sure you had any good black socks, so I went ahead and
bought these for you. And here is a handkerchief," Michiyo said,
taking the items out of a shopping bag. "I checked all your drawers
to be sure you had enough clean underwear. I'll stay for a few days
to help the new maid."

Shunsuke nodded.

He heard the voices of the people there. In fact everybody seemed
to be talking to him. Out in the yard, the dog was barking, not
having been fed. Shunsuke was about to ask Ryoichi to feed the dog
when he heard Michiyo telling the maid to do it.

Shunsuke went into the kitchen and couldn't keep himself from
blurting out: "The water's been running in the bathroom. The well
water's turned brown. Someone has to keep an eye out when we
have this many guests. The floor plan of this house makes people
congregate in the living room, but since it's right next to the kitchen

with only a curtain dividing them, everything said in one room can be heard in the other. An odd design for a house, even if looks nice . . . But it's not good for us, and it's not good for the guests to hear everything . . ."

The new maid looked at him sharply, then lowered her head.

"It's so hard for you to do everything without your wife, Mr. Miwa," Michiyo said. "If you were younger, or older, maybe it would be easier. I'm sorry about the water, but we'll manage." Then she turned to the maid and said, "Just bring those empty teacups down here, please."

"Yes, right away."

Michiyo seemed to be supervising the new maid well.

Thinking of his daughter suddenly, Shunsuke called out, "Noriko! Noriko! Where are you?"

"She's in the tatami room," answered Shimizu, who'd been staying at the house, in a loud voice.

"Oh, Shimizu, thank you for your help," Shunsuke said, his voice dropping. "I wonder who's going to stay with us tonight."

"Don't worry. I will. But this house, Mr. Miwa," Shimizu went on, "is just like a hotel. People tend to stay in different ends of it."

"That's why the living room was designed the way it is, to get everybody in one place."

Here again, the topic is this house, thought Shunsuke.

"Well, I think it's fine if you stay for one night, but having been here for a week, I don't think it's the easiest house to relax in. Somehow, with all these closed windows, it makes you feel like you're suffocating. I now understand what you meant in the article you wrote in the art magazine."

Shimizu's comment made Shunsuke tense.

"Wouldn't it better to sell it and buy a smaller house?"

Shunsuke looked straight at Shimizu, as he always did when he was speaking to someone about the house. "I can't do that."

"Why not?"

Shimizu's face was there right in front of him, revealing his uncomplicated personality full of good intentions.

"Why? Because if I sell it now, I'll lose money."

"Isn't it to your advantage to sell it when it's new?"

Shunsuke was close to tears.

"People have said that it was because of your wife that you built this new house. Now that she's gone, maybe you should think about getting rid of it? It's presumptuous of me to say these things, but I mean well and you should know that other people have been saying the same thing."

"But this is my wife's house . . ." Shunsuke realized he didn't know what else to say.

All of the friends who were gathered in the living room had been of help to Shunsuke at one time or another—whether it had to do with the children, the houses, or money. Shunsuke had done the best he could to return the favors. But for several years these friends had not come to visit him at home. Hearing that many of them shared Shimizu's opinion about the house was disheartening; it made him resentful.

౼

The next day, a few of Tokiko's and Shunsuke's friends came to the house to sit for the wake. Ryoichi sobbed occasionally, and seeing that, Noriko giggled. After the service, Shunsuke went into the tatami room, where the women were sitting.

"Poor child, you will be so lonely," Michiyo was saying to Noriko, holding her in her arms. "You'll soon be the age when a girl needs her mother most. You'll need advice for all kinds of things. I feel such sympathy for you. When I saw your mother at the hospital, she talked about this more than once."

Did she really? When? Shunsuke wondered.

Noriko started to cry. Shunsuke couldn't bear to see his daughter looking so miserable. Michiyo shouldn't be saying things like that to her, he thought as he walked away; it's inconsiderate.

Shunsuke felt desperate. Just then, Noriko came to him, no longer crying.

"I'm all right now," she said. "I feel sorry for Mom, that she had to die . . . I'm OK about the other stuff, really. Mom would be so upset, though, if she knew Michiyo and those other women were pitying her."

"That attitude of Noriko's isn't helpful," Michiyo was saying to the new maid. "She should let herself cry. Feeling sorry for her mother sounds like a kind thing, but it's best to cry your heart out at a time like this. Noriko is just like her mother, you know. Mrs. Miwa had a certain presence, and she liked to take care of other people. She'd always been in good health. She was the person who had this house built, and if she hadn't gotten ill, she would have made certain there were no leaks. Mr. Miwa, he is a quiet and gentle man, but he'll throw a fit once in a while. Noriko might have gotten that from him, not that she actually throws fits."

Shunsuke went upstairs and found some of his friends in his room, sitting on his bed and looking out through the large window. Shimizu was among the men there.

"True, the view from here is splendid. You can see Mount Fuji quite well. But it must be unbearable in the summer with the afternoon sun."

"I like this house," responded Yamagishi, who was colleague of Shunsuke's. "Contemporary style is my ideal. I like functional modern buildings. Mr. Miwa sleeps and writes here in this room."

"Noriko sleeps here now because she's frightened by the sound of the trains at night," Shunsuke said. "When they go through the valley over there, the sound is particularly loud."

"I wouldn't mind staying with you for a while. This house is too big for just the three of you. It must make you lonely," said Yamagishi.

"Yamagishi might be the right person," said Shimizu, smiling.

"Do you really think so?"

"He's single, and he lived alone in America for many years. He can be very rational. Besides, you've had an American staying with you on and off, haven't you, Mr. Miwa? I think Yamagishi would be perfect to keep the family company." Shimizu turned toward Shunsuke, looking concerned. "Michiyo is very capable, don't you think?" he said, changing the subject. "Everyone seems to like her, and she's been quite helpful, knowing exactly what to do. When no one thought of it, she asked for money to pay the new maid for the extra hours she'd worked. But why did she stop working for you, Mr. Miwa?"

"She's got arthritis."

"She's been helpful, but she sure puts me to work," said Yamagishi.

"Someone has to stay with us, someone outside the family," Shunsuke mumbled to himself.

⌒

When Tokiko's seventh day of memorial services was over, Yamagishi brought his things into Noriko's room with Ryoichi's help. He rearranged the desk so that he could do his work, stacking his books, dictionaries, and papers neatly. He coughed, moved a chair around noisily, and muttered to himself in English, acting as if he was in a hotel room.

Yamagishi mainly stayed and worked in his room. He would go downstairs to take a shower or to have tea with Shunsuke in the living room.

Ryoichi, who insisted on sleeping in the room next to the living room, got out of bed around noon and carefully studied the new lodger. Noriko, still absent from school, stayed upstairs.

Shunsuke observed his household, particularly Ryoichi and Yamagishi, from a distance. At the same time, he had a sudden feeling of attachment for everyone, even the dog. When no one remembered to feed the dog, he let him bark, watching him through the window. If Ryoichi didn't attend to him, Shunsuke would do it, pretending he just remembered. Once, in the darkness, the dog jumped on him, frightening him.

༞

The new maid wanted to quit. Working for a family without a mistress was too difficult, she said. Shunsuke thought right away of asking Michiyo to come back.

"Mom said she's slovenly," Noriko objected.

"She would be better than a stranger," said Ryoichi. "It's easier with her because she knows how Mom did things. I hate being asked at two o'clock every day what I want for dinner. Anyway, you said you don't like to have a stranger meddling in the kitchen. If that's the case, Michiyo would be better."

"She better not start talking about Mom, or start pitying me . . . Because if she does, I'm definitely going to complain. After all, I have rights as the daughter of this household. You don't like her, though, do you, Dad?"

"Well . . ."

"You don't have to like her. I think it's better to have someone very different from Mom," said Ryoichi, puffing on a cigarette.

My son feels the same way as I do, thought Shunsuke. He knew he needed to have Michiyo around, so that he could get back at her. As long as it's all right with Noriko, Shunsuke announced, Michiyo will do.

༞

Two days later Michiyo started working for them again.

"Please tell me, all of you, whatever you want me to do. I'll work just as hard as I did when Mrs. Miwa was alive," she said, bowing to the three Miwas.

"We want you to do everything the way Mom told you to. We leave it up to you," said Ryoichi.

"She lives within me," Michiyo replied. Then she went to the altar, took the urn in her arms and started to mumble and sob.

"Where will she be buried, Mr. Miwa?"

"We don't have a plot in Tokyo."

"We bought one in Tama. Why don't you find one somewhere nearby? Then I would be able to visit her often."

"That's true," Shunsuke said unenthusiastically.

"Let's not talk about gloomy things. I don't want to hear about Mom now," said Ryoichi.

"You look young in that colorful skirt, Michiyo," Shunsuke said.

"Don't tease me, Mr. Miwa."

"But you seem pleased," said Ryoichi.

"Well, I'm a bit nervous. On the day of the funeral, I showed only my best side, you see."

"Don't worry," said Noriko, "we all know that."

"I really tried hard, thinking that Madam was watching me. Without her I may not be good."

Shunsuke laughed out loud.

⌒

Several days later, having asked his daughter first, and making sure Yamagishi would be home, Shunsuke went out. Standing on the platform at the station, however, he started to worry, mainly about Noriko. What is she doing now? Is she thinking about her mother? When he left the house and walked down the street to the station, he had felt free, released for a couple of hours. As he walked, keeping his eyes on the trees with leafless branches, drab dried-up grasses, and houses and streets that looked so ordinary, he realized he was walking, and seeing things, in a manner that resembled Tokiko's.

I am a man who has just lost a wife, he said to himself as he glanced at the women on the street. Soon, his eyes had changed to those of a mother, someone like Tokiko, who had left her children at home.

Standing on the platform, he found himself thinking that he had felt far freer in the house. Now he wasn't sure where he wanted to go. He stood watching the woman working at the kiosk; he felt like crying.

It occurred to him that he hadn't paid the hospital bill; he had been carrying the money around in his pocket for the past few days.

He went to the hospital, paid the bill, and received a condolence gift of a thousand yen from the hospital. Then he walked to the department store, taking his usual route.

In the store, beyond the crowd of shoppers, he saw the mannequin now in a different robe. Beside the mannequin was a woman in the familiar store uniform, gazing blankly at the customers.

This tranquility of despair, the longing, and the sweetness that melts away, Shunsuke murmured. The feeling nearly made him choke.

The saleswoman had a broad nose; her small, round face and her long, sloped eyes gave the impression of being out of balance. When she talked, she moved her lips to one side. Why am I studying this woman so calmly? Shunsuke wondered. What am I so desperate about, and why do I gaze at this woman as if I have spotted prey? Checking that the other salesclerks were busy, Shunsuke approached the woman. The moment she smiled at him, he could tell she didn't recognize him.

"I want to buy that robe for my daughter," Shunsuke said, pointing to the mannequin.

The woman seemed taken aback.

"That one over there, I want it," he continued.

"That one?"

"My wife died," Shunsuke said, then smiled faintly.

Shunsuke told the woman that wanted to talk to her and that he would wait for her by the entrance at closing time. He pulled out money out of his pocket and placed it on the counter. She could bring the robe to him at that time, he said. He then ran down the stairs instead of taking the elevator.

Around six-forty, Shunsuke spotted the woman in the crowd of people leaving the store; she wore a dark green overcoat and was looking around for him. As he took the shopping bag from her, Shunsuke asked where she wanted to go. The moment he said it, he knew he was doing it all wrong. He felt dizzy, as he often did when he'd said the wrong thing to Tokiko. It doesn't matter where, said the woman, eyeing him cautiously. I don't like this expression on her face, Shunsuke said to himself, and then the woman mentioned a coffee shop nearby with a French name. I'm letting you decide what you like, he thought.

"Where do you live?" Shunsuke asked with sudden tenderness after they were seated. He was absentmindedly thinking about something else, and yet he was scrutinizing her body, her hair, her fingers. Everything about her made him despair. Not because she was unattractive; he felt despair for no particular reason.

"I live in a dormitory. But what is it that you want?"

"What do I want . . . ? Are you single?"

The woman nodded, looking angry; she fidgeted in her chair.

"Excuse me for asking, but how old are you? I mean, to tell you the truth," he stuttered, thinking what he was about to say was something he had never said to any woman before. "I am very fond of you, therefore . . ." He felt a meanness in him just then. "Where is this dormitory?"

"It's in Suginami."

Meeting a woman like this is pointless, Shunsuke was now thinking. He should leave, go home. But the woman was becoming more responsive.

"How many of you share the apartment?" he asked, even as he had begun to think this: I must take care of the garden. The trees that were planted when the house was built have been left unattended; overgrown branches will damage, even kill, them. The water in the pond will soon freeze, and unless something is done, the ice will kill the goldfish; it might worsen the crack in concrete, too . . . Then water will seep into the ground, and if that happens, the foundation of the house will be affected; unless the dirt is held tightly, it'll wash away, and the dirt on the hill might slide down, and the house built on a slope will collapse, crashing into the house below . . .

"Are you seeing someone at the moment?" he asked, while reflecting upon the answer she had just given him, that she shared an apartment with two other women. He fantasized about how he would marry this woman, how he would be a matchmaker for her two roommates. When he came back to reality, he discovered that the woman in front of him was different from the woman in his reverie. This made him want to cry. The real woman in front of him was saying something.

The coffee shop was crowded with people looking for seats. Whenever he spotted a woman entering, he looked at her intently. He wished he could get away from the woman sitting in front of him, but at the same time, he thought he had to continue telling her how interested he was in her.

Suddenly, the woman stood up. Shunsuke picked up the check hurriedly and followed her to the door. Outside, he saw her walking toward the train station, and beside her was a young man, trying to get her attention. The man then turned around, looking in Shunsuke's direction. Had that young man been inside the coffee shop, or was he waiting outside? Shunsuke didn't care. He stood there watching the woman walk away, feeling she was someone who had nothing to do with him. Only a few minutes ago he wanted to go home right away, but he felt differently now. Why? The feeling that he had no place to go was intensifying. I feel I'm nobody unless I'm with the children and Yamagishi, he said to himself, twisting his lips. And that house . . .

On the train, Shunsuke felt eager to get home, as if he was trying to escape from something, as if there was an important task awaiting his return. Why am I not ashamed of what I've done, he thought. And why do I think I have achieved some sort of vengeance? If it was vengeance, then on whom? On himself, or on someone else? Am I on the verge of tears because I am sad? Tokiko shouldn't have died . . .

౷

Walking home from the station through dark streets, Shunsuke looked up his house on the hill and saw that the only light in the house was in Yamagishi's room.

"On that night, Tokiko, you came home from the PTA meeting and you'd had something to drink. You came straight to my room, and you told me, 'Tell me you want me, and be convincing.' Remember that? Still in your good dress, you fell on top of me, and you said, 'Go ahead, do it.' I was lying under you. Unless you keep your eye on me, I'm going to get myself in trouble, I said to you. You looked shocked and became more insistent.

"Then there was the time we went to a bar with my friends. George had just started coming over to the house. You had a drink, and a friend of mine asked you to dance with him. When we got home, you told me, 'You're quite civilized now, not getting upset at my dancing with another man.' You said so even though you'd never danced like that before with anyone . . ."

"He was you. You were George, you see. I couldn't explain it, but that's what it was."

"Was that how it was?

"Yes, it was. So it was nothing, really. Just a man and a woman sleeping together."

"I won't get upset now no matter what you do."

"Because I'm dead?"

"No, not because you're dead. Not because you've been so sick and suffered so much . . . Tokiko, don't talk in such a sweet voice . . ."

"Well, I'm not sure it's not because I'm dead. You can't fool me, you know. But you've lost weight, and you look slimmer than last year. You ought to thank me for that. Your chest used to stick out like a woman's. You look quite good now. Let me see you . . ."

"Hey! Don't tickle me like that!"

"What are you giggling about? Twisting your lips like that. And your smile, looking so shy. Now don't be so pathetic. Go ahead and sleep with her. Why not? She's only a salesclerk. Why, you're embarrassed! Don't be bashful. Look, your face is all red. Even your earlobes are blushing. Come children, look at your father! Ryoichi! Noriko! Come look!"

Shunsuke heard the dog barking. It had probably not been fed. Yamagishi should take over the job and manage the house, Shunsuke thought. Like an American housewife. He should keep the house in good order, not just tidy up his own desk, run the vacuum clearer, or take a shower. In the morning, he should wake up Ryoichi; it's a job an outsider can do with less friction. And Noriko . . . I wonder how she's doing . . .

Entering the house, Shunsuke saw Ryoichi's and Noriko's shoes lying in the foyer just as they'd been kicked off. Shunsuke, still thinking about his expectations of Yamagishi, tried to decide whether he should straighten the shoes or not. Now that he had to be in charge of everything, paying attention to these matters was necessary. He was going to run his household the way he saw best. That was good in theory, but in practice he had no idea how he would accomplish it. Suddenly, he felt drained.

In the living room, he found the children sitting with their heads close together.

"Where is Mr. Yamagishi?" he asked, although he knew the answer.

"Never mind about him, Dad. Where have you been?" Ryoichi said, standing up. "Your dinner is on the table, getting cold."

"You sound just like your mother," Shunsuke snapped at his son.

"You're the one who sounds like Mom. And I don't care where Yamagishi is. You don't need to concern yourself with trivial things like that. Act more like a father."

Shunsuke felt misunderstood. "Why are you so upset?" he said to his son. "I thought you enjoyed talking with Michiyo."

"Enjoy? I'm doing it for everybody's sake," Ryoichi responded. "When I tell her about girls, she gets interested and wants to talk with me about them. But the truth is, I can't stand her cooking. Besides, when I say something to tease her, she thinks I'm flattering her, and she misses the point. At her age, she still wears all that makeup. It's Yamagishi's fault. He flatters her all the time."

"Stop it, Ryoichi," Noriko interrupted. "I know you have something to tell Dad, and you're angry because you know what he'll say. Dad, he wants to move out."

Ryoichi wanted to share an apartment with two friends. He pulled out a sheet of paper that he'd scribbled down monthly expenses on. His share of the rent would be nine thousand yen.

"Mr. Yamagishi agreed to stay with us partly for your sake, Ryoichi. Besides, Mom's ashes are still here, unburied," said Noriko.

Ryoichi was grinning now, a grin that resembled Shunsuke's. When he saw his own expression on his son's face, Shunsuke had the momentary illusion that he himself must have turned into Tokiko.

"Your mother wouldn't approve," he said.

"Yamagishi is here, so I thought it would be all right for me to move out."

Just as Ryoichi said that, Yamagishi came down into the living room.

"Why do you want to leave, Ryoichi?" Shunsuke continued, feeling encouraged by Yamagishi's presence.

"I feel oppressed."

"Oppressed? What makes you feel oppressed?"

"I can't explain it."

"You can't explain it? But you don't just move out because you feel oppressed. That doesn't make sense. What do you think, Yamagishi?" Shunsuke said, feeling triumphant.

"Well, I can't say, and I don't know about other people. But it seems, Ryoichi, that you should listen to your father."

Shunsuke expected Ryoichi to scream, just as Tokiko had done at times like this, but instead Ryoichi, not knowing what to say, laughed quietly.

"You are responsible for the future of the Miwas, too, my older brother, and you'd better remember that," Noriko chimed in.

"If that's the case, can I bring a friend to live here with me?"

"Do you feel oppressed, or are you lonely? Which is it?" asked Shunsuke with a smile on his face. Next, Ryoichi might say that he doesn't like the sight of me, he thought;, now that Tokiko is gone, he's the one who has to put up with my sour face. But your face looks just like mine now, he wanted to say to Ryoichi.

"Go ahead, if that's what you want," said Shunsuke, feeling gentle and generous all of a sudden.

"We'll use Mom's tatami room, then. You can stay in my room upstairs, OK Yamagishi?"

"Sure, I don't mind," Yamagishi said, looking at Ryoichi, then Shunsuke, smiling. "I kind of like that room."

When Shunsuke and Noriko were getting ready to go to bed, Ryoichi came into their room and sat down on the bed.

After a bit, Shunsuke said in a low voice, "I think I'll get married again after all."

"I don't like that," Noriko said right away. "Definitely not,"

"But it was your mother who suggested it," said Shunsuke.

"Of course she did. She had to." Noriko's voice was unexpectedly spiteful.

"Noriko's right," Ryoichi said. "Besides, we don't know what kind of person you'll marry."

"Why don't you just have an affair, Dad?" asked Noriko. "But don't bring any women here. I couldn't stand seeing the face of another woman in this house. I can barely tolerate Michiyo. Since Mom died, she's always looking at me like she pities me. I bet she's happy I don't have a mother, because now I can be her daughter. She thinks I don't behave properly or something; I can tell. Maybe it's not her fault, but that's the way I feel."

"It's worse if he has an affair, Noriko. We don't want him to forget about his responsibilities at home. We'll be in trouble if that happens," said Ryoichi.

"But Dad has needs, too. Of course I don't want him to have an affair, but an affair is better than him getting married. Don't you see that?"

"You seem to know everything. If you're so smart, why aren't you sleeping in your own room? Why are you here in Dad's room?"

Noriko ignored him.

"It's not that I want to marry again for my own sake. I prefer to remain the way we are. Because I can feel your mother is with us. But if you two never leave the house, or if I think only about you, that wouldn't be good either."

"Maybe," Noriko said rather sharply, "but I can't think about it now. It's too cruel for Mom . . ."

She won't cry, Shunsuke thought. But is she all right like this? Noriko did not cry.

ノ

The family had received many gifts of condolence. Shunsuke deposited half the amount in the bank, and the other half he made into a check, which he took to the hospital and handed to the doctor. Shunsuke would write a letter of thanks to everyone and explain how the gift was used.

The doctor, a little embarrassed, thanked Shunsuke and said he would have the hospital administrator send him a receipt. "Your wife's tumor is preserved in alcohol," the doctor added. "And this is the report on her case. The progression of her illness and the treatment are shown on the graphs here. I'll send you a copy when the report is done."

Shunsuke pretended that Tokiko was still alive, recovering in the hospital.

As he was leaving the hospital grounds, Shunsuke heard lively voices coming from the direction of the tennis court. Turning around, he saw Dr. K and his nurse, Miss Nishimura, playing a doubles match. Shunsuke stood and watched as Nishimura hit the ball, shouting as she did so.

I should start seeing Nishimura, he thought.

⁓

Shunsuke had often met her when he took Tokiko to the outpatient clinic. Sturdily built with broad shoulders, Nishimura had a square face with a fair complexion. Shunsuke used to look into Dr. K's office, and if Nishimura was there, he'd indicate that he and Tokiko had arrived. "Hello, Mr. Miwa. I'll call you when we're ready for you," she always said. With that, Shunsuke would go back into the waiting room, but every time she came to call the next patient, he would stand up. "Please, this way," she'd say. "No, not you, Mr. Miwa. In a little while." Shunsuke would feel grateful at this and he would say, "Yes, thank you."

Once in the examination room, Shunsuke would stand by Tokiko, watching her and hoping the examination would be over quickly, before she became exhausted. "The examination won't be much longer," Nishimura would tell him, knowing his concern. Sometimes, she would say, "Doctor, let's get this done quickly." And, to Tokiko, she would say, "Oh, how are you feeling? Are you having chest pains?"

Nishimura was very good at bridging the gap between doctor and patient.

The first time Tokiko was hospitalized, it was Nishimura who took them to her room. "I'll leave you here," she said. "The floor nurses don't like me fussing around. Please take good care of yourself." One day, at the outpatient clinic after Tokiko's first discharge from the hospital, Shunsuke struggled to lift Tokiko up when her turn came. "Wait a moment, Mr. Miwa. I'll help. I'll be there in a minute," Nishimura called out. Everyone in the waiting room was watching. "All right, Mrs. Miwa, let me help you," Nishimura said when she returned. She was able to get Tokiko upright with one hand propping up her lower back. She then guided her into the examination room. Shunsuke followed, filled with gratitude. Whenever he heard her say "Mrs. Miwa," tears welled up in his eyes.

"She needs a private nurse, Mr. Miwa," said Nishimura when Shunsuke rang one day to see if Dr. K would make a house call. "Her situation is not good . . . She should not have left the hospital . . . It seems she's had a relapse, but there's no way we can send a nurse . . . Didn't the doctor give you instructions? Sometimes we forget, but . . . And she's in pain and coughs a lot? What? Did your neighborhood doctor really tell you to give her that medicine? How much? Oh, no, she shouldn't take more than 0.5 milligrams. Any more than that and it'll make her feel worse."

At Dr. K's office, Shunsuke asked Nishimura to arrange to have someone from Dr. K's staff visit Tokiko at home. He also asked her to arrange Tokiko's readmission to the hospital. Nishimura did not smile even once.

As Tokiko's condition worsened, Shunsuke began to view Nishimura as personifying Dr. K. He had come to believe she knew the truth, while the others could not be relied on.

"Does your wife's personality seem to have changed? Has she become very dependent?" Nishimura asked him. "You have to watch these things. My father was just like that."

Shunsuke had nodded.

↵

He called the hospital at nine-thirty in the morning. He knew that Dr. K would not be at the office yet: that Nishimura would be readying patients for their examination. The thought that she was busy helping other patients depressed him.

"Mr. Miwa? Oh, yes, Mr. Miwa, you're the husband of our late patient. How are you?" Nishimura answered in her high-pitched voice. "I'm very sorry about your wife. You must be so lonely."

"I want to thank you for everything. When is your day off?"

"Sunday, of course."

"I want to see you very much. I must see you in fact," said Shunsuke off the top of his head. His heart was pounding as if he was confessing to a lover.

"See me? Oh, dear. But thank you for asking . . ." The sound of her cheerful voice filled the space.

"To tell you the truth, my late wife told me if I could find a woman like you, I should . . ." Shunsuke almost said. Instead he said, "Can I see you next Sunday then?"

"It would be very nice to see you, but I can't promise you now."

"By the way, those blue pills prescribed for my wife, can I take them when I feel upset?"

"That'll be fine. There're no side-effects."

"Good. Well, then, I'll call again, perhaps on Saturday."

"Please take care of yourself."

Shunsuke put down the receiver and stood there in a stupor. He was not at all pleased.

He didn't call Nishimura again.

↵

The friend that Ryoichi brought to live with the Miwas had also lost his mother recently. Kizaki was his name. The two boys slept in Tokiko's room.

Shunsuke was the first to get up in the morning. He warmed up the bathroom for Noriko, who suffered from constipation because of nervous tension, and made her a bag lunch. Hearing activity in the kitchen, Yamagishi, who awoke at five o'clock, came downstairs and tried to wake the two boys. It was a thankless task, but Shunsuke had asked him to do it.

At the breakfast table, Shunsuke watched his daughter eat with her face lowered, surrounded by four males. Kizaki also kept his eyes on his plate, and Ryoichi wore his usual sullen expression. Yamagishi seemed oblivious to Ryoichi's sullenness. Shunsuke kept his eyes on Yamagishi, who, having lived abroad for ten years, knew how to stay detached, not involving himself in other people's business. That must be how he is able to live in this house, thought Shunsuke.

Yamagishi was, in fact, a model of comportment. He would ask Noriko how she was feeling, but he did so merely for the sake of asking. Noriko knew this, and she would answer accordingly, annoyed at the whole exercise. Kizaki detected this unhealthy atmosphere permeating the house, and Ryoichi, knowing this, worried.

Every morning Yamagishi set the table with dishes, knives, and forks. Then he would announce, "Breakfast is on the table, everybody." Even after Michiyo had returned to work, he kept this routine up. A great many dishes were put out, washed, and put away. Shunsuke, Noriko, and Yamagishi did the dishes at night. Yamagishi's system was to throw everything into the sink. This irritated Shunsuke and Noriko, who felt that it somehow jeopardized the order of the house.

All through this, Ryoichi and Kizaki sat and smoked.

During the day, they would spend most of their time lying on the living room couch. This is where they slept now, not in the tatami room. Seeing this, Shunsuke grew angry, as Noriko could not go into the living room if Kizaki was lying on the couch.

Shunsuke talked to Ryoichi about this, and Ryoichi, who didn't want to say anything to Kizaki, stopped lying on the couch himself, hoping his friend would get the message. This only lasted for a few days.

If Kizaki is to be criticized, Ryoichi said, then so should Yamagishi. "I don't know if his is the American way, but it looks like a mixture of American and Japanese," he complained to his father. "He always looks after himself first. Besides, he's never been married, so he doesn't know what it takes to run a household. Kizaki's not used to life in the city, and he doesn't understand many things. So I have to explain to both of them, and that's a drag. It's a real burden, and I can't sleep at night. Then it's hard to get up in the morning. When Yamagishi comes to get me up, he's horrible. I bet he thinks he's the one who runs this house. In fact, he is using your room, isn't he?"

Shunsuke listened to his son without comment; somehow, this made him feel more alive. You're right, it is hard to run the house, Shunsuke wanted to tell his son, and you should know that that's what your father has been doing.

"I don't know what's going to happen to Noriko," Ryoichi continued. "She's beginning to talk like a man, and she's stretching herself beyond her capacity. Do you think that's good for her? She can't sleep well either, so it's hard to get her up in the morning. You, Yamagishi, and Kizaki don't seem to have that problem. Kizaki thinks he's a good guy because he can get up; he tries to wake me up, he says Yamagishi has called several times already. He wants to impress Yamagishi. We didn't have this problem when George was staying with us. Because Mom was here."

"Why do you bring up George now?" Shunsuke muttered, not knowing what to think.

"But it's true, isn't it?"

"How so?"

"How? Don't ask me. It's you who wanted him to live with us. Because you'd been to America, I guess."

"That's not true."

"Not true? But you didn't object. Mom did what she thought you wanted."

Shunsuke said nothing.

Ryoichi, who was waiting for an answer, said, "Well, that's over."

"Noriko can sleep in her own room now," Shunsuke said.

"But she says her body shakes, and her knees make funny noises, things like that. The same thing happened to me when my body was growing. I wonder if she should have a friend live here, too."

"No, she can't."

"Bringing someone into this house from the outside makes it harder to manage, I can guarantee you," Michiyo shouted from the kitchen.

"I still think Noriko should invite someone to come to live here," Ryoichi went on. "It's best if Michiyo takes over all the chores, including waking us up. She can go ahead and scold us, too, but she'd have to live here."

"I don't mind staying over once in a while," said Michiyo, joining the conversation.

"Once in a while isn't enough."

"I can't do that because I'm not your wife, Ryoichi. You should go ahead and find a wife. If you want me, I'll take good care of you. Actually, it's a good idea for a younger man to marry an older woman."

Ryoichi laughed and said, "Ask Yamagichi if he's interested."

"I wonder if he's mature enough. What do you think, Ryoichi? What's your opinion, Mr. Miwa?"

"Why don't you ask Yamagichi?" said Shunsuke.

"I may be outspoken, but I wouldn't do such a thing."

"The frying pan is burning," said Noriko, who walked into the kitchen just then.

Ryoichi decided to have a Christmas party and invited his friends. Yamagishi and Kizaki helped decorate the living room, and Michiyo and Noriko made sandwiches. Yamagishi brought over his stereo from his apartment, then went to Akihabara with Ryoichi to buy colored lights to brighten up the room.

When she finished preparing some other dishes for the party, Michiyo put on her good dress, and when the guests arrived, she greeted them like a bar hostess would. She danced with Yamagishi, giggling, and then, saying she'd come early the next morning, left without cleaning up. Shunsuke heard her saying good-bye loudly to the guests.

⁓

Noriko had sought refuge in her room, and Shunsuke went up to see her. "Come, Noriko. This is your house, too. Don't just watch other people have a good time. Go ahead and dance. Laugh and enjoy yourself. I'll dance, too."

"I don't want to."

"Why are you so stubborn? You're just like your mother, but she was crazy about dancing in the end."

"I'm more like you."

"Then I'll dance."

"You can do whatever you like. It doesn't matter if you're good or bad at it. I still don't want to."

"Well, then, go ahead and cry if that's what you want to do."

Noriko's face tensed up, and soon she started to sob. She cried with all her energy. Shunsuke wished she wouldn't cry like that. It wouldn't do her any good; it could even hurt her.

"You go downstairs first, Dad," she said. "I'll come soon."

"All right, but you should come because it's for your own good."

The moment he stepped out of her room, Shunsuke heard Noriko lock the door. He was taken aback. "OK, you're going to cry. Go ahead and cry as much as you want," he said and realized he had uttered the same words Michiyo had.

Noriko made no reply.

"You'll come down in a while, won't you? If you have a personality like mine, you should try to correct it."

"I'm more like Mom," Noriko shouted, and started to wail. "Don't worry, I'll come down," she then said between her sobs.

"If you don't dance, your mother will be upset."

"Now you're pestering me."

"Pestering? I see," Shunsuke muttered, thinking how Noriko was like her mother after all.

"You're crazy."

"OK, if you say so."

Shunsuke went to his room, and threw himself on the bed, anxiously waiting to see what his daughter would do.

Half an hour later, the door of his room opened, and Noriko walked in stolidly.

"I served tea to the guests earlier . . ." she began with her eyes to the floor, averting Shunsuke's gaze.

"Tea?"

"And I spilled some . . ."

"Oh, that . . ."

It was because no one took the tray from her, and when the tea spilled, the girls all stood up.

What is it that occupies this young woman's mind? This daughter of his, who'd matter-of-factly tell him when she was having her period, what her body odor was like. This person, who said that her body grew each time she moved, that she worried her hormones were out of balance, like her mother's. It'd been more than a year since she was deprived of a mother's care and attention. This was his daughter, and her bodily changes were occurring daily, which was almost frightening.

". . . And then, Mr. Yamagishi said something about my putting too much tea in the cups. On occasions like that, he takes the woman's side. So he said things to make the girls feel good. I suppose what he meant to say was that the spill was no big thing. But I don't think they really wanted to hear that either. He thinks all women want to be flattered. 'You must be at least 170 centimeters tall,' you heard him say that to one of the girls—didn't you? He said that deliberately, to insinuate that I'm short. Even Michiyo chimed in with something."

"Mr. Yamagishi tries to be accurate, that's all. He's not aware of how people feel. Westerners have their own ways and customs, but you can't be natural acting like they do unless you grow up that way. When Japanese try to practice Western customs, we still use the Japanese language, so it doesn't work well. It only puts you off, and everyone else. It's the same the other way around."

Noriko nodded, but Shunsuke thought she might not have been listening.

"I feel sorry for Ryoichi. Mr. Yamagishi told him they're his guests, and so he should do a better job entertaining them. Ryoichi was busy making cocktails. He can't do everything at once. I feel we've been humiliated in our own house. I don't know what will become of us."

"You don't want to dance, then?"

"I'll dance after everybody's gone. I'll dance by myself."

Shunsuke left his daughter alone and went downstairs.

⌁

Once Ryoichi and Kizaki had seen their friends off and Yamagishi had retired to his room, Noriko and Shunsuke put on a record and started to dance; it was the twist.

Hearing the music, Yamagishi came back downstairs. "Noriko," he exclaimed, "you're very good! I can't do it like you do."

"It's easy, Mr. Yamagishi. Anyone can do the twist. Just like this. Don't be shy. Try it," said Noriko softly, glancing bashfully at Shunsuke.

࿚

Later, when she was about to go to bed, Noriko said to Shunsuke, "Dad, I think I should be more independent and responsible. But sometimes I get confused and say things that you would."

"Is that why you locked your door?"

"Yes, but I'm not sure. It's partly because Mom's gone, but I don't think much about her now. When you peek into my room, though, it's a little hard. You were the one who said I needed to become more independent. I think you're right."

Shunsuke was shocked at what his daughter was saying.

"It's not your fault, Dad, but I think I understand what Mom was saying now."

"What did she say?"

"She said it made her uneasy when you looked into her room. But, Dad, I'm not criticizing you. Maybe you're just timid."

Shunsuke and Noriko were facing each other in the darkness at the top of the staircase. Noriko is not capable of what's most important, which is idle small talk, he was thinking. And that'll make her reticent and not easily liked, even cause her to ruin her marriage . . .

"Noriko," he said softly so that Yamagishi would not hear, "you should tell me everything, anything, whatever is on your mind. Just as you used to with your mother. About your clothes, friends, your teachers. Anything." As he spoke, he was overwhelmed by a sense of helplessness and wretchedness.

࿚

"It's unreasonable to expect her to tell you everything, Mr. Miwa," said Michiyo the next morning, smiling.

"But she's getting used to telling me everything . . ."

"Still, she's a woman."

"Well, of course, I'm not a mother or a housewife."

"Upsetting yourself like that is bad for you, Mr. Miwa."

With the urn containing Tokiko's ashes still in the house, Shunsuke felt unsettled, though for no clear reason. One morning, he hired a car and along with Yamagishi went to take the urn to a temple. The children were still in bed, and Michiyo did not volunteer to go with them.

Shunsuke had never been to this temple, which the hospital mortician had recommended. The temple faced a huge gas tank, and a railroad track ran through the cemetery. The priest escorted Shunsuke and Yamagishi to the shrine, which was across the railroad track. The priest lifted the gate and opened the door to the shrine, where fifty or sixty urns were neatly placed on the shelves. He cleared a space for the urn Shunsuke was carrying. The urn cannot stay here forever, Shunsuke thought. He would have to buy a plot somewhere.

"I can see that you've been totally dependent on your wife," Yamagishi said gently.

"Me? Why do you say that?"

"Well, because you seem to be at loose ends."

"More so than other people, would you say?" Shunsuke asked, surprised. "If so, it's not because I was dependent on her."

"Well, it doesn't matter. By the way, Shimizu said Dr. K called and asked how you were doing. He sounded quite concerned. I told Shimizu you were fine," Yamagishi said.

Shunsuke nodded, but what he wanted to say was that he was only doing what was expected of him. If a casual remark like that affected him this much, he worried that his home might be in danger of disintegration.

"Ryoichi also told me he found it upsetting, seeing you at such loose ends. But I told him this was normal, to be expected."

"Did Ryoichi say that? So that's why you used that expression. Now I understand. Well, you don't have to worry."

This was exactly the role I've wanted this man to perform, Shunsuke thought. That's why I asked him, a stranger, to come and live with us. But I am definitely going to have to find a wife. How, though? He was beginning to feel desperate, and this business of finding a new wife was developing into something of an obsession.

~

Ryoichi, who continued to be sullen, told his sister that he wanted to leave the house. When Shunsuke heard it from Noriko, he noted the fact that Ryoichi hadn't told this to him. Feeling that he would explode, he said nothing and merely observed his son.

Late one night, loud noises could be heard downstairs, and as Shunsuke lay awake in bed, he heard Ryoichi coming up the stairs.

"Noriko, come. Mom's down here!"

Angry, Shunsuke jumped out of bed. He found Ryoichi standing at the top of the stairs with a blank expression on his face.

"Don't wake her up. You mustn't tell her things like that. Come here. Why didn't you wake me up?"

"Why?" Ryoichi looked at him blankly and then stammered, "But she was standing in my room. When I left my room, she was in the hallway, too."

"Where is Kizaki?"

"He went out."

"Well, he shouldn't have. We asked him to stay with us for times like this. It was a dream, Ryoichi."

"No, it wasn't a dream." Ryoichi stood still, in a daze.

"Then, I'll go and see myself. In fact, I'll be glad if it's your mother. We're having a tough time around here. What is it that she has to say?"

Shunsuke stomped down the stairs ahead of his son, looking dead serious.

"There's no one here."

"But I saw her. She was there."

"Can't you tell a dream from reality?" Shunsuke barked, switching the light on.

When they came back upstairs, Yamagishi was standing in his pajamas outside his room.

"It was a dream. I had a dream like that once. I was in America and I had a chest cold and I was feeling lost. My mother appeared and sat on my bed, praying to the Goddess of Mercy. When I said, 'Mother,' she turned around and looked at me with the same awful expression she would use when she was scolding me. It was strange that I had such a dream since in those days I never thought about the Goddess of Mercy. But dreams like that are fairly common."

"How old were you when you lost your mother?"

"I was in my second year of high school."

"What happened to your father?"

"He became irritable. I hated seeing him like that, so when he remarried, it was a relief."

"What was your mother like?"

"My mother? She was from a good family, and she kept my father under her thumb. She had tuberculosis and was confined to bed for many months. She did things like hit the maid with a measuring stick. Seeing that was pretty upsetting. She was sent to sanitarium very far away, and I took the train to go see her, but I was told to go home. I was very sad."

"And your father remarried?"

"Yes. Three months after my mother's death. But you're a very different man from my father, Miwa."

Kizaki, who had just returned home, came upstairs and joined in the conversation.

"Your mother died about six months before mine, didn't she?" Ryoichi asked him.

"Who does the cooking at your house?" asked Shunsuke.

"Mainly my father. My sister helps. My grandmother's been doing it for a while, though."

"What's your father like?" Shunsuke asked. "I mean, what do you think of your father?"

"Me? I respect him."

The moment he heard this, Shunsuke hated Kizaki.

"You don't have to worry about that kind of dream. Besides, no ghost would haunt a brand-new house like this," said Michiyo, who, hearing everyone, had also come upstairs, wearing a short robe over her nightgown. She was staying the night because her son was visiting a relative and she didn't feel safe being alone. "I still dream of my dead husband," she went on. "I have to laugh because in my dreams he's quite handsome. He lived for three years, half-paralyzed, after he had a heart attack in the bathroom. It was what he deserved for gambling on the horses. But one hundred days isn't enough time to let a dead person go. You'll feel different in a year, I assure you. After three years, my son and I were even able to talk and laugh about him in front of his picture."

An unexpected feeling of closeness descended on the small gathering at the top of the stairs.

༄

The following evening, Ryoichi went to Shunsuke and asked for a monthly allowance of 35,000 yen so that he could get his own apartment. He didn't want to see Yamagishi's face anymore. The man, he said, was not contributing to the Miwa household; he was only making life difficult for everyone. Having Kizaki around was an additional burden in the house without a housewife, he added.

Shunsuke could not help but smile when he heard the words, "thirty-five thousand yen" and "housewife."

Thirty-five thousand yen amounted to just about the expense of having Yamagishi and Kizaki around, Ryoichi said. So he wanted that money.

"You're crazy," Noriko said. "It won't last, and you'll be right back. If you want to leave the house, you should find a job. That's what Dad means by 'independent.'"

"You know that's not possible."

"I bet you'll go live with a woman. That'll make you feel like a grown-up. Then it's us who will suffer. It'll affect my marriage prospects, you know."

"Don't act like you know everything," Ryoichi said, laughing.

When Shunsuke said he didn't approve of this plan, Ryoichi was silent for a while. "If that's the case then, can I build a little room underneath the balcony and live there with Kizaki?" he asked.

"Go ahead if that'll make you feel better. But plan carefully and build it by yourself," said Shunsuke, thinking how his son was just like Tokiko.

⁓

The next morning, when the two boys were on their way to buy shovels, Shunsuke admonished his son not to start without planning carefully.

No problem, Ryoichi responded.

As soon as the boys got back, they started digging. Shunsuke went out to help, and also asked Yamagishi to pitch in. The four of them worked on removing the soil for the next two days. Shunsuke noticed that Yamagishi was sulking, but he ignored this.

Ryoichi asked three other friends to help, and they all slept over. When the digging was done, the foundation of the house was exposed. A workman had to be called in; he reinforced the foundation and finished the room. When the work was all done, and while waiting for the paint to dry, Ryoichi suddenly stopped talking; he spent the day lying on the couch in the living room.

"I don't know what Ryoichi is thinking, but you and he have a lot in common," Yamagishi said to Shunsuke, sounding amazed. "You once said this house was built against your wishes, but actually it was you who built it. This time, too, you saw that the extra room was completed even though you weren't in favor of it at the beginning. I now understand the mechanics of the Miwa household."

"This sort of thing isn't so uncommon; it happens in many families. And it's you who caused it, you know."

"I can't agree with you there," said Yamagishi.

"What else can one do? It's different, of course, if you have a great deal of self-confidence, but not many of us do. For example, on what grounds would you object if your wife had an affair? There aren't any good reasons to object, really. Sure, you'd be irritated, but all you can do is to look for some ways to eliminate the irritation."

"I don't quite follow you," Yamagishi said.

Shunsuke was sorry he had brought it up.

What Ryoichi says is outrageous, but there are times when I feel I understand him right away, completely, as if water has seeped into me, and I'm filled with the feeling he's talking about, thought Shunsuke.

～

After a few days passed, Shunsuke asked everyone in the house, including Michiyo and Kizaki, to come to the living room. He had something to discuss. He wanted to know what they thought of his remarrying. He himself preferred not to remarry, but what did they think?

"I think," said Ryoichi, "I think we're all suffering because there is no housewife in this house. Since you'll get married again anyway, the sooner the better."

Noriko and Kizaki proposed, in response to Noriko's complaint about Ryoichi's laziness, that Ryoichi could be in charge of such chores as the household finances, planning the meals and telling Michiyo what to cook, as well as keeping track of things like the heater and air-conditioning. That way the extra cost of Yamagishi's staying with them, which was the point of Ryoichi's complaint, would be covered, and Ryoichi would have something to do. Ryoichi, who was at first flabbergasted at the proposal, seemed willing to consider it.

It was Noriko's turn. "As I said before, I'm against Dad bringing any woman into this house."

"Stop talking nonsense, Noriko. Think of how lousy it is for me," shouted Ryoichi. "Dad is thinking of marrying again because it's good for everyone. He has no other reason."

"If Dad thinks it's best for him, I won't object to it. Because if he's not OK with it, all of us will sink," Noriko answered with deliberate slowness.

"Don't you think Mr. Miwa exaggerates the need for a housewife? Don't you think so, Michiyo?" said Kizaki.

This surprised Shunsuke, and he stared at Kizaki.

"I agree," Michiyo replied, "but what I think isn't important. I'm just an employee. I know I can't please everyone all the time. I'm not very capable, not like Mrs. Miwa."

No one responded to this, and Noriko turned her face away.

"I somehow thought you weren't going to marry again, but if you do, I'll leave of course. I do I like it here, though," Yamagishi said.

"What I'm trying to say is that I'll marry if it's good for Ryoichi and Noriko," said Shunsuke, looking at his children. "I don't know how it'll work with this person, but I will make sure she's someone you like. I know it's not easy, but it'll be better for all of us to try."

"It doesn't work unless everyone tries hard. It won't be easy, that's for sure," Michiyo said.

"Come to think of it, that's not such a crazy idea," said Yamagishi.

"That's right, Dad. You should go ahead and do it. Go ahead, Dad," Noriko said playfully. Everyone looked at her.

"Men have it easy. Even at your age, you're able to find a wife," Michiyo said.

Although this discussion was his idea, Shunsuke began to find it unbearable. "I'm not going to do it right away. I thought you should know that I might," he said, hoping to end things.

But why do I become so eager, as if I am seeking vengeance on someone? he wondered. Am I seeking vengeance on that salesclerk? or on Nishimura, the nurse? Why, furthermore, do I think that only women who have little hope, who have missed their chance of marriage, are candidates to be my second wife? Shunsuke wanted to run out of his house and cry out—he was not sure about what. Did I ask everyone to gather here because I wanted to cry out in front of them?

When he retired to his room, Shunsuke lay down in bed and wept, pressing his face against the quilt.

"May I come in?"

It was Yamagishi, who wanted to ask Shunsuke a few questions about a translation Shunsuke had given him to do. He had a problem with tense, he said, because the past tense in English and Japanese seemed to carry different nuances.

All translators are aware of that difficulty, Shunsuke told Yamagishi. A way to get around it is to convey the nuance through some other means. Having explained that, suddenly Shunsuke felt better.

"In this novel," Yamagishi continued, "the professor leaves his wife for a month to teach a summer course because he wants to buy a new car for her. When he returns, he finds something has changed in his wife. Their children sense the change, too, and express it in terms of the fragrance of a flower in bloom. The husband presses his wife, and she confirms his suspicions. The husband kicks her out of bed. The wife commits suicide, the husband kills her lover and then himself. But the lover is his older brother, and before he dies, the brother admits his guilt but says it is the husband who is most responsible. He asks the husband which will he choose—the book or the pistol?"

"'The book' refers to the Bible," Shunsuke said.

"Yes, I understand that. In the end the husband commits suicide, leaving a son and a daughter behind. Realizing what has happened, the children experience a great deal of pain, but the story ends with a hint that they will start living their own lives with hope."

"That's not how things end up in real life," said Shunsuke.

"My point is that these Western characters act logically here. That's what I think. Compared to them, the Japanese are temperamental, vague, and opportunistic."

"Westerners don't always act logically either. Not like the characters in this story."

"But they try, because otherwise people can't communicate with each other."

"What we've learned from the West is often in conflict with our traditions. We suffer from the outcome of those conflicts in our homes. You'll see when you're married."

"I won't get married until I'm ready. But do you think remaining single keeps a person from being whole? I rather doubt that myself," said Yamagishi. "The problem about being single is what to do about sex. It's not easy in Japan for unmarried people. America's a bit like that too, but in France, even married women are a lot freer. I like that." Shunsuke didn't know what to say.

"I don't think you're going to marry for sex, but do you really want to be married again?" Yamagishi said.

Shunsuke nodded, thinking that Yamagishi was becoming too persistent. If Shunsuke was serious, Yamagishi then said, he knew a woman he might wish to meet. But he wasn't sure how the woman might feel, even if Shunsuke liked the idea of meeting her.

ぐ

The next day Shunsuke called several old friends. He told them that he wanted to marry again and that he needed their help. His first call was answered by a friend's wife. After a brief silence, she said she would consult with her husband.

Another call was also answered by the wife, and again there was silence. She then said that it wouldn't be easy—not because of him but because of the children.

Yet another call was made to a friend of Tokiko's, who said she had anticipated this request. It shouldn't be too soon, but not too late, either. It requires very careful consideration, she said.

Each time he spoke to someone, Shunsuke said something like, "since the children agree with me," "as I can't do without a wife," or "I wouldn't if it weren't for the children." He did not notice any anger in voices of the women he spoke to, but that may have been because he was close to tears.

*

A letter arrived from his friend Shimizu: "People are saying that you are overly preoccupied with your family and are inconsiderate of the feelings of others; they think you shouldn't be making phone calls like that. And one more thing, it's impolite to donate the condolence gifts to the hospital." The letter urged, in carefully chosen words, that Shunsuke exercise more discretion.

*

"What happened to your plan of getting married again? The photo of the woman Yamagishi showed you looks all right to me," Ryoichi said on a day when Kizaki had gone back to his own home.

"You're not the one who's getting married," Noriko said.

"You should go with Dad to meet her," Ryoichi retorted. "You liked her in the picture. Go and see her." The woman was thirty-six years old, an illustrator, a little plump with large eyes and a wide forehead.

"She looks nice," both children had said earlier.

࿔

Shunsuke arranged to meet Yoshizawa Chikako at the same coffee shop in Shinjuku where he had gone with the salesclerk. Yamagishi was to be there; Noriko went along too.

Entering the coffee shop, Shunsuke saw a woman in the far corner nervously watching the door. She looked frightened. When Yamagishi introduced her to Shunsuke, she smiled, but her body grew even more tense. Shunsuke started talking to her as soon as Noriko and Yamagishi moved to another table.

First, he asked if she was busy. She was, she replied; because she wasn't a first-class illustrator, she couldn't afford to be choosy about projects, and she needed to earn enough to support herself. "I tend to be accommodating and flatter people, but I can be quite frank, too," she added, looking at Shunsuke as if she held a grudge against him.

If she married, did she intend to quit work? Shunsuke asked. If not, how much time would she like to devote to it?

She didn't know.

Shunsuke started talking about himself, suddenly on fire. He was about to mention the bedroom they might share, but stopped himself in time.

"And then . . . ?" the woman was saying.

Shunsuke changed the subject abruptly. "If you marry me, would your family suffer financially?"

"Oh, no. They would be glad. Both my younger brother and my mother complain about my not leaving the house."

Then why does she hesitate? Shunsuke thought.

"Seems like you're saying 'yes.' Am I right? My children liked your picture, and I'm sure that Noriko is glad to meet you today."

"She's not sure about giving up her work," interrupted Yamagishi from the next table.

"I know," murmured Shunsuke, disheartened. "My children are not hard to get along with," he went on.

The woman looked up at Shunsuke fearfully, and he saw shadows under her eyes. She must be tired of being single, he thought.

"Miss Yoshizawa," he said, calling her by her name for the first time. "You may be worried about getting up in the morning since you work at home. What time do you get up now?"

"Around eleven. Then I fix something to eat. When I'm home in the evening, I cook dinner, but most of the time I'm out, meeting with people about work."

Shunsuke was quiet for a moment. "Well, I guess it's all right if you sleep in at times," he said eagerly. "After all, what's important is that you stay at home."

He gazed at her neck, conjuring an image of their being in bed together. Could I handle her well, stay calm yet be energetic? Maybe. I mustn't antagonize her. How would she look when she got up at eleven in the morning? But I don't care about that. I did say I don't mind if she gets up late, so why is she hedging? Does her reluctance indicate her distaste for my family? I can't let her despise us because if she does, I will hate her—and everybody else as well . . .

Shunsuke motioned to Yamagishi, and the four people rose to leave. When Yamagishi held the door for Yoshizawa and Noriko, they almost bumped into each other. Yoshizawa was letting Noriko go first, but Noriko thought the older woman should go first.

"I'm so clumsy," Yoshizawa apologized.

They walked for a while and stopped at a shoe store for Noriko. Shunsuke let Yoshizawa help Noriko choose what she wanted.

"You have small feet, Noriko," said Yoshizawa, slipping her foot into the shoe Noriko had taken off.

One down, one to go, thought Shunsuke, shifting his eyes to

women passing the store. Women are walking, women are walking, he mumbled to himself.

～

Back home, Shunsuke asked Noriko and Yamagishi what they thought.

"I don't know . . . I like her eyes, and I think she's honest," said Noriko. "But she only talked about herself."

"She's starting to go to seed," said Yamagishi. "She's been single too long, and she's lost her courage. She'll be all right, though, once she's married. It's a common trait of women who've never married."

After Noriko left the room, Yamagishi announced his verdict to Shunsuke: "I think she should marry you and move in. But the greater question is, why did you go to meet her? What was the reason? Do you know?"

Shunsuke was perplexed, not sure what Yamagishi was getting at. You can't possibly understand what I'm feeling, he thought.

"You went to see your late wife," said Yamagishi.

"I tried to be sensitive. I tried to be deferential."

"I know that's what you think, but you came across like you were talking to your wife. The marriage won't work if you're going to be like that."

Shunsuke was surprised to hear this. "What did Yoshizawa say to you?"

"She doesn't plan on getting married right away."

"This isn't good. What could she be worrying about? This isn't good for us."

"She says she's scared of Noriko."

"That's ridiculous," Shunsuke laughed.

"Noriko's gone through a lot. Of course, she can't compete with Noriko."

Shunsuke was irritated. "I'll call and meet her again."

"She has a lot to think about, and she feels she doesn't understand you."

"Me? I explained a lot to her. I thought she was nice person."

How arrogant of her, thought Shunsuke. He'd only ever felt this way about professional women and bar girls.

⌁

Hearing from Shunsuke that the woman had no intention to marry yet, Ryoichi stared at his father accusingly. "Then when does she want to get married?" he said. "And what about our situation here? What's Yamagishi doing?" He threw himself on the couch and started leafing through a magazine.

Shunsuke was furious, but said nothing.

⌁

Shunsuke had forgotten about Yoshizawa. But then, out of the blue, he took her picture out of the envelope and stared at it. He became angry and felt like grabbing her by the neck and dragging her into his house.

It was several days before he could see her again because she was busy. On the phone, he was annoyed at her having to consult her calendar, and yet he spoke to her courteously.

She is very polite when she greets me, Shunsuke thought, sitting down in a coffee shop; she's sitting there as if this is a confrontation with me and my family. He decided not to talk about himself.

"I understand you're not sure, but there's nothing for you to worry about."

Yoshizawa sniffed. Too many cigarettes, thought Shunsuke.

"Do you think I'm a silly woman?" Yoshizawa began. "My parents say so. I get up late, and even when my mother comes to wake me, I deliberately don't get up. Do you think a person like that is worthless?"

"As I said, you needn't worry. I can tell from your eyes. You're timid, that's all."

"I am timid and passive. Lately, I seem to be even more withdrawn."

"As I said, you don't have to worry about that. With my children it will be good, being like that. Your personality is what counts."

"But don't you agree that there's something I lack?"

What is this woman getting at? Shunsuke wondered.

"Listen to me, please. Of course, you can remain single, but if there's a chance to marry, I think you should take it. I'm telling myself the same thing."

What is this woman here for anyway?

"Well, apart from the matter of marriage, do you think I am a worthless person?"

Shunsuke grabbed the bill and stood up.

Walking toward Shinjuku Station, he felt strong emotions surging up inside, which propelled his hand toward her. "You'll be fine," he said to her, pulling his hand back before it touched her buttock. He was shocked at himself. Other than in intimate moments, he had never touched a woman's buttocks.

At the train station, Yoshizawa ran up the stairs. Watching her, Shunsuke felt angry.

　　　　　　　　　　　⌒

Yoshizawa Chikako phoned Shunsuke next. They had a few drinks, and then went to a coffee shop. Besides apologizing to each other for the other day, they spoke of nothing in particular.

Then Chikako said, "My mother told me to ask you what you think about me."

This made Shunsuke feel like he was being challenged, and it prompted a little hostility. "As I already told you, if you like my children, I think I will have affection for you," he said.

"But I would be marrying you."

Any favorable feelings Shunsuke had toward her evaporated at that moment.

"The first time I saw you," Chikako went on, "I thought your eyes looked like fish eyes."

"Fish eyes? What do you mean?" Shunsuke asked, upset at hearing this.

"Well, they had a sort of vague look to them. But they don't seem that way now."

࿐

As they made their way back to the train station, Chikako offered to carry Shunsuke's briefcase. He declined the offer a few times, but then she offered to carry it with him. When he agreed, she said, "I'm quite used to carrying heavy things."

As her train was pulling up to the platform, Chikako declared, "I think we're rushing things. Besides, there are many women who are better than me." Then, having boarded the train, she turned and bowed to him.

Shunsuke stared at her. When she looked away, her expression revealed a gloominess that he had never seen in her before.

࿐

When he returned home, Shunsuke went straight to his room. He paced restlessly. Then he picked up the phone.

"Miss Yoshizawa, this is Miwa. What are you doing right now?"

"I've just told my mother everything."

"You are at a crucial point of your life. You face the choice either to be a real person or not," he shouted into the mouthpiece.

"I need more time to think about this objectively."

"You'll stop talking like that if you come to live with us. If you don't, you'll go on living exactly the way you are now. Why don't we try and work together? I assure you I am ready; I don't think it's premature. If I wait any longer, my family will fall apart. Then it'll be impossible for the person who comes here. Whoever that may be, it's going to be very hard. But tell me, why did you offer to carry my briefcase? and to pay the bill? So you wouldn't owe me anything? And you said I have the eyes of a fish. But what I'm feeling is something holy."

Shocked at his own words, Shunsuke hung up the phone. Vacantly he looked around his room.

He went downstairs, where a French song was playing on the stereo. Yamagishi and the children were sitting and reading. Michiyo, who was spending the night again, came in with a stony expression, carrying a tray with tea.

"If you want to forget the whole thing, that'll be fine with me," said Yamagishi, "but I suspect you'll marry just so that you can make that person miserable, whoever it is."

"That's not true. That might have been the case before, but I've learned," Shunsuke said. But, Shunsuke wondered, did I really abuse Tokiko? If it's true, wasn't it because I was longing for genuine human contact?

He looked at Ryoichi and Noriko sitting together.

"I've decided against marrying this woman," Shunsuke announced.

"What?" they cried. "That's not good."

"I want you to bring a housewife in here soon," Ryoichi shouted.

"Things don't happen just like that, Ryoichi," said Michiyo, drinking her tea. She then twirled off into the kitchen coquettishly.

⌒

Someone touched his face, and Shunsuke, in bed, struggled to open his eyes. He was having difficulty breathing, and he cried out, just as Tokiko had when she was in pain, "My chest! My chest!"

"Mr. Miwa . . ."

When he finally opened his eyes and propped himself up, he saw Michiyo, standing in her nightgown in the dark near his bed.

"Mr. Miwa," she said again.

He jumped up and stared at her.

For a moment, he thought he might as well give in. But instead, he dashed to the wall where the light switch was. In the brightened room he saw that Michiyo was displeased. He saw that she was breathing hard.

"Go back to your room, please," Shunsuke said, remembering that Michiyo had once said to him that she was not that kind of shameless woman. He realized he might have been waiting for this moment.

"I asked you to go to your room," he said again.

"I'm not like your wife," she said defiantly.

He had let this woman come back into his house in order to turn the whole incident around, to make her forget about it. But, he said to himself, if she's going to talk like this, I might as well pull her into bed.

"Ryoichi has gone, Mr. Miwa."

"Gone?"

"I heard noises, so I went to his room and found this note. I think it's best for him to try to make it on his own."

Shunsuke pushed Michiyo out of his way and stormed into Ryoichi's room. Then he looked out through the window at the dark veranda. His heart was pounding. He went downstairs and put on his shoes to go out, banging into the large glass wall panel. Some guests had mistaken it for a doorway before, but this was the first time for Shunsuke.

"Next it'll be Noriko . . ."

He didn't think Noriko would actually leave home, but then . . .

Once outside, Shunsuke ran down the slope. The dog started to bark.

I've got to get rid of Yamagishi, Shunsuke thought. No, I'll let Michiyo go first . . .

SELECTED DALKEY ARCHIVE PAPERBACKS

FOR A FULL LIST OF PUBLICATIONS, VISIT:
www.dalkeyarchive.com

SELECTED DALKEY ARCHIVE PAPERBACKS

FOR A FULL LIST OF PUBLICATIONS, VISIT:
www.dalkeyarchive.com